D0677799

"No one has ever injured on my watch."

Jesse wasn't sure why Abby was telling him this. "I can appreciate that."

"Eighty percent of the people I guide up here are men, and every single time, I have to prove myself and be questioned in a way that my brothers never are."

Now he knew why she was so upset with him. "I'm sorry I questioned your choice."

"It's just that it gets old after a while. What I did back there probably kept us alive."

"I never should have dragged you into all this. It's just that I couldn't get up here on my own. I would have died."

"Well, whether I like it or not, we're in this together. I can't in good conscience just walk away from you, and I kind of think those men would kill me just as fast as they'd kill you."

He felt a rush of gratitude toward her. "Thank you, Abigail."

"I will get you off this mountain alive."

Ever since she found the Nancy Drew books with the pink covers in her country school library, **Sharon Dunn** has loved mystery and suspense. Most of her books take place in Montana, where she lives with three nearly grown children and a spastic border collie. She lost her beloved husband of twenty-seven years to cancer in 2014. When she isn't writing, she loves to hike surrounded by God's beauty.

Books by Sharon Dunn

Love Inspired Suspense

Dead Ringer
Night Prey
Her Guardian
Broken Trust
Zero Visibility
Montana Standoff
Top Secret Identity
Wilderness Target
Cold Case Justice
Mistaken Target
Fatal Vendetta
Big Sky Showdown
Hidden Away
In Too Deep
Wilderness Secrets

Texas Ranger Holidays

Thanksgiving Protector

WILDERNESS SECRETS

SHARON DUNN

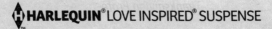

HARLEQUIN® LOVE INSPIRED® SUSPENSE

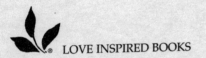

LOVE INSPIRED BOOKS

ISBN-13: 978-1-335-23185-7

Wilderness Secrets

www.Harlequin.com

Printed in U.S.A.

Trust in the Lord with all thine heart; and lean not unto thine own understanding. In all thy ways acknowledge him, and he shall direct thy paths.
—*Proverbs* 3:5-6

To my Lord and Savior, counselor and king,
who makes all things new and is a God of second chances.

ONE

Fit to be tied.

That was the phrase Abigail Murphy's grandmother had used, and it was how she felt right now as she stalked toward the trees that would lead her back to civilization. The weight of her backpack seemed to increase as she hiked. Abigail adjusted the shoulder straps, lifted her chin and tried not to obsess over the notion that her client—Jesse Santorum—had not been completely forthright with her. As a wilderness guide, she worked with all kinds of people. But Jesse had gotten under her skin.

It had taken three days to hike up to the remote area where Jesse said he wanted to fish. He'd been tense the whole time, insisting that they put in long days to get to the destination. But once they stood on the shores of shimmering Crystal Lake, fishing seemed to be the last thing on his mind.

Four days ago, when Jesse had walked into the office of Big Sky Outfitters, his request had seemed strange from the get-go. He needed to be guided into the lake, but he didn't require her services to be guided out. He'd been up-front with her about not needing to get him back out, but usually when a client wanted to improve their skills, they asked that the guide stay close in case they got lost.

She would have refused his request if it hadn't been the off-season, if this hadn't been the first time she was left alone to run the business while the owners, Heather and Zane, had gone on their honeymoon. She wanted to prove to her new employers she was worth her salt. Though she'd worked as a guide since she was a teenager in Idaho, she was new to this part of Montana.

Being a female guide meant she was always in a perpetual state of having to prove herself, anyway. She'd taken the crisp hundred-dollar bills Jesse had fanned out on the desk and made him sign a waiver that Big Sky Outfitters was not responsible if he got lost on his way back into town. She'd taken all the precautions. She'd left him with the satellite phone in case he did need help.

Then she prayed her bosses would be happy with her decision and nothing disastrous would come of it.

Abby pulled herself from her negative thoughts and took in her surroundings. She was only a few yards from the edge of the forest.

Five crows fluttered up from the edge of the trees. Their wings flapped in the breeze. Something had scared them.

Abby stopped as the hairs on the back of her neck stood at attention. She listened. Maybe an animal had alarmed the birds. Her heartbeat revved up a notch. This high up in the mountains, it could be something as benign as a deer, or as dangerous as a mama bear with cubs. Because it was spring, the bears would be coming out of hibernation, hungry and looking for food. She didn't want to be a bear appetizer today.

She turned back to look up at the mountain peak, where Jesse said he was going to hike to get the *lay of the land*. Those were his actual words: *lay of the land*. What did that have to do with fishing?

She clenched her jaw. She was no longer responsible for him. Why, then, did she feel like he wasn't telling her the whole truth? Why did it make her so mad? Maybe it was just because her trust in men had been broken to pieces in the last month.

She was still raw from her breakup with Brent. After three years and an engagement ring, he had started dating another girl in the church choir behind her back. When Brent got the job with the US Forest Service, she'd followed him out here to Fort Madison with the promise that they would be married within six months. She'd left her family and the small town in Idaho where they'd both grown up for a shattered dream.

Abigail stomped closer to the tree line, unable to shake off the tightening in her chest. Stupid Brent. How could she have been so naive? *Just because a man holds a girl's hand in church every Sunday doesn't mean he'll be faithful*. At least she'd dodged a bullet and found out before they were married. Tears warmed her eyes and she sniffled. That didn't make the heartache go away.

She glanced one more time up the mountain where Jesse had gone. She couldn't see him anymore. She had half a mind to go up there and demand an explanation. She turned and took several more steps toward the trees.

Let it go, Abby.

This was just about the pain of the breakup. Pain too easily turned to anger, and she was considering taking it out on the person in closest proximity, namely Jesse. She stomped forward. Getting into an argument with a client was never a good plan.

If he wanted to navigate himself down the mountain, fine. If he had never intended to go fishing, fine.

The truth was, she had never experienced betrayal at the level of Brent's. Her father had been a good man, a faithful man who had taught her everything about wilderness survival, just like he'd taught her three older brothers. Her throat tightened, and she swallowed to push down the heartbreak that kept nagging at her.

Would she ever be able to trust a man again?

She stopped abruptly when she heard a noise coming from the trees. A sort of rustling and moving around, almost indistinguishable from the other forest sounds. Animals were usually stealthier as they moved through the forest.

And then a sound that resembled a grunt reached her ears.

Her breath caught. Her heart pounded.

That didn't sound like a bear or a deer. The noise was human.

DEA agent Jesse Santorum perched on the mountain peak and drew the binoculars up to his face. At this high point, he had a view of the landscape down below to the west and to the east. To the west, he saw the woman who had guided him up here headed toward the trees. Abigail Murphy walked with a determined stride despite the weight of the pack she carried. Even at this distance, he could see her long blond braid flopped over the backpack. She walked with such intensity, almost like she was mad.

Though he'd been up-front with her, she'd seemed agitated that he only required her services to get him to this point. In fact, she had been a little huffy toward him for the three days they'd been together. She seemed distracted, as well. At one point, she'd led him down the wrong trail, and they had to backtrack several miles.

He hated not being totally honest with her about why he'd come up here, but he had no choice. For her own safety, it was better that she didn't know the real reason he was in these mountains. He'd needed her expertise to get to this remote location. He told her only part of the story to keep her out of danger.

The truth was, he had a different way to get out other than hiking. He turned and stared through the binoculars to the east. Camouflaged with tree branches, the downed drug plane was right where Lee Bronson, another DEA agent, had said it would be. If he had told Abigail about the plane, it would have made her a target. The cartel would stop at nothing to get information out of people.

He had a pilot's license. His plan was to fly the plane out. It was Lee's fingerprints all over the drugs, not his. The hard drive that contained the original photographs and audio tape that Lee had doctored and given to the DEA was in there, too.

While they'd been running an operation down in Mexico, Lee had been hit with a fatal bullet. His dying confession was that he had framed Jesse for the drugs he'd stolen. Now the DEA thought Jesse was the turncoat, and the cartel was after him for the drugs Lee had taken for personal gain. He'd gone rogue, not knowing who would believe him at the agency and who would turn him in. Agents in the field who worked with Jesse knew his character, but he was uncertain how much Lee had poisoned the higher-ups in the organization against him. If he had evidence, he might be able to clear his name.

He glanced back down to where Abigail was about to disappear into the trees. She stopped and lifted her head, as though she'd heard something.

Two men emerged from the forest and grabbed her, dragging her back into the evergreens.

His heart squeezed tight as he bolted up from his hiding place. He grabbed his handgun from the back-pack where he sat it on the ground, and raced down the mountain. He'd sent her away to protect her, to en-sure her safety.

Maybe those men who'd gone after Abigail lived up in these mountains and would be aggressive toward anyone because they weren't used to people.

As he sprinted around the rocks, navigating the steep incline with ease, he realized that a showdown with crazy mountain men would be a best-case scenario. At the back of his mind, he wondered if the cartel had tracked him to Montana because they desired revenge and wanted their product back.

Oh, God, let that not be the case.

He slowed down as the terrain leveled off, seeking cover behind rocks and bushes. He entered the forest. With his weapon drawn, he pressed his back against a tree and listened for any sound that might be out of place.

He took in several ragged breaths and then moved deeper into the forest. His heart drummed in his ears and his muscles tensed, ready for a fight.

He swiped any images of violent things happening

to Abigail from his mind. He was no good to her if he let himself be distracted by his own fear. He needed to use the fear to focus, to stay strong, to keep any harm from coming to an innocent woman like Abigail.

With his gun raised, he took one careful step forward. A sort of crashing sound to his right caught his attention. He eased toward where the noise had come from. Through the trees, he saw a flash of movement and color.

He stopped when he heard voices.

A male voice said, "You two are in this together."

"I don't know what you're talking about." Abigail's words were filled with anguish. "I was hired to guide him up here."

Jesse pressed his back against a tree and closed his eyes. This was the exact opposite of what he wanted to happen. He had to get Abigail away from these men.

The same male voice responded, "You're protecting him."

"No, I was hired to do a job. That's all I know," she said.

"You will take us to him," the other man shouted.

Why hadn't Abigail said that she'd last seen him going up the ridge? Was she trying to protect him at the expense of her own safety?

"Please, let me go. I don't know anything. I dropped him off by the lake. He was going to do some fishing. I don't know anything. Who are you, anyway?"

"We ask the questions."

The second male voice piped up. "I bet we can use her to lure him out."

Jesse squeezed his eyes shut and gripped his gun even tighter. How dare they use her as bait?

"How do we know he's not sitting in the cockpit of that plane?" asked the first voice.

"Nothing's shown up in the sky yet. Besides, he's not going to leave his partner behind."

"I'm not his partner. I told you that. Please, just let me go. I won't say I saw you."

Jesse stepped a little closer to assess exactly what he was dealing with. He crouched and moved toward the voices, one careful step at a time. When he was close enough, he hid behind a tree and peered around it.

There were three men. One of them held a rifle and wore a backpack. His job appeared to be guarding and watching. He walked the perimeter around Abigail and the other two men.

Jesse's heart squeezed tight when he saw Abigail on her knees, her head down. They must have dumped her backpack somewhere. At least she wasn't tied up.

Both of the men standing over her were muscular and probably in their twenties. One of them had pulled a handgun from a holster and paced back and forth in front of Abigail. His hair was dark and slicked back, and he had a tattoo on his neck.

The other had bleached blond hair and a deep tan. He reminded Jesse of one of those men who appear on the cover of romance books at the checkout counter, kind of a pretty boy. He, too, had a gun, but it was not drawn, and their two backpacks were propped against a tree.

How was he going to get in there and rescue her?

"We would have been able to track him to the plane if Eddy here hadn't gotten lost." Pretty Boy pointed at the guard.

The guard—Eddy—spoke up. "You wouldn't have gotten anywhere without my skills." Eddy had a low, deep voice, and every word he spoke seemed to contain a threat.

Jesse assessed that Eddy was probably the most dangerous of the three men. He saw murder in his eyes. But the dark-haired man appeared to be the one in charge. The neck tattoo, a scorpion, meant that these men were connected to the drug trade.

A plan sparked inside Jesse's head. He stepped back from the unfolding scene, then ran as fast as he could. When he got some distance away, he shouted, "Abigail, where are you?"

He bolted from the clearing where he'd made himself known, running in a wide arc back toward the men holding Abigail. Hopefully, at least one of them would run to find him. Then he'd have only two men to deal with.

He heard one man shout something at the other, their voices getting farther away. He came toward the area where Abigail was being held. Sure enough, only Pretty Boy had been left to watch her.

He waited until Pretty Boy's back was turned, leaped into the clearing and hit the back of his head with the butt of his gun. The man crumpled to the ground.

The voices of the other two men drew nearer. From their angry chatter, it was clear they realized they'd been tricked.

Jesse grabbed Abigail's hand. Fear was etched across her features.

"You're coming with me." He pulled her to her feet and sprinted away.

As he pushed through the trees, he let go of her hand. The steady pounding of her footsteps told him she was keeping up.

The voices of the men grew louder, filled with rage. One of them barked orders at the other two. Abigail and Jesse neared the base of the mountain peak that would lead them to the plane.

Jesse glanced over his shoulder. The man with the rifle, the one they called Eddy, had ditched his backpack and was taking aim with the rifle.

The rifle shot pummeled the silence.

Abigail did not even stutter in her steps. She only increased her pace, so she was now running beside him.

There was a cluster of evergreens at the base of the mountain that provided them with a degree of protection. He slowed, tiring from the intensity of the run and needing oxygen. Then he stopped altogether to take in a deep breath.

She quit running, as well. Sucking in air between each word, she asked, "Where are we going?"

"I have a plan. Trust me."

Her face blanched, and a curtain seemed to fall over her eyes. "*Trust* is the biggest word in the English language."

Pain seemed to undergird her words. There was no time to consider what was going on with her emotionally. "Those guys are out to kill us. I can get us out of here." He touched her elbow. "We need to keep moving."

He pushed himself off the tree he'd been leaning against and sprinted through the evergreens.

She followed behind him. He stayed in the trees, trying to get a little more distance between them and their pursuers, before they could veer back out in the open and head up the mountain.

They had to get to that plane and get it off the ground

before the thugs caught up with them. It was their only way out.

He burst out into the open, where the incline grew steeper. At first, they were able to keep up a solid pace. But rocks and the cliff-like slant of the mountain slowed them, so they were climbing more than running and had to reach out for handholds as well as stable places to put their feet.

Rocks rolled down the incline, crashing into each other. This was much tougher going than how he had initially climbed the mountain. The peak was not even visible yet. He craned his neck, scanning the tree line below, half expecting to see Eddy with his rifle.

It appeared that Eddy had not followed them into the trees. That fact was troubling. It meant Eddy and the others might be headed up the mountain on a different route. Maybe one that would get them to the peak faster. They risked being ambushed.

The plane was camouflaged enough that it was not easily spotted from a distance. He doubted that even if the men got to the plane first, they would leave him and Abigail alive. They were witnesses. If Lee had set things up to make Jesse look guilty to the DEA, he might have been feeding lies to the cartel, as well.

As he was dying, Lee confessed that his plan had been to sell the drugs slowly, so as not to draw attention. It made sense that if he didn't want to be looking over his shoulder wondering if the cartel was after him, he would have Jesse take the fall for him. Lee had started to explain more, but he'd died before he could finish.

No, these three thugs would not leave until they

knew he and Abigail couldn't talk. This wasn't just about getting their product back. It was about revenge for being crossed.

TWO

Abigail's leg and arm muscles burned as she reached up toward a rock that looked like it was stable. "This is getting too steep. We can't climb much farther without gear. We need to move that way." She pointed south.

Off in the distance, she saw the forest where Jesse had helped her get away from the three men bent on violence. Though she didn't see the men anywhere now, the memory of what she'd just been through made her shudder.

"Is there some other way?" asked Jesse. "Those men are probably going to be coming from that direction."

Even though her heart was already pounding from the adrenaline and exertion, it sped up even more from uncertainty. What was going on here? She could not process what had just happened.

Who was Jesse, anyway, and why were those men after him? Why did they think she was somehow involved in whatever had really brought him up here?

"We'll be stuck here if we don't move laterally. It only gets steeper if we head north." She didn't wait for his reply before she stepped sideways, seeking less treacherous ground. "I assume we're moving up this mountain to get to the plane those men mentioned?" Her voice was filled with accusation.

She didn't trust Jesse. She didn't know what he was up to. The only thing she knew for sure was those three men wouldn't flinch at killing her. And Jesse had risked his own safety to get her away from them. Getting to that plane seemed like the only way she would make it out alive.

Jesse didn't respond to her question about the plane.

All of this felt so wrong. How had she gotten into such an ugly mess? Why hadn't she trusted her gut feeling about Jesse, that he was up to something? Because the person she trusted the least right now was herself.

After Brent's grand deception, the new rule she operated under was that nothing was as it appeared. She wasn't a good judge of character.

Even though Jesse had risked his own life to get her away from those violent men, it didn't mean he wasn't a criminal, as well.

She walked carefully on the rocky, steep terrain until it leveled off a little bit, allowing her to climb upward. There were fewer rocks and jagged cliff faces and more grass on this part of the mountain. Even a few struggling junipers, trees that were more like bushes, dotted the landscape. Their tangled trunks and branches grew low to the ground. The breeze ruffled her hair as she focused on moving up the mountain. Silence surrounded her.

Then Jesse dived to the earth, taking her with him. Her stomach collided with the hard ground. She felt the weight of his hand on her back. "What's the big idea?"

"They're down there," he whispered. He rolled away

from her and crawled toward a juniper tree, peering through its branches.

She slipped in beside him. Two of the three men, Eddy and the blond man, huffed up the mountain at a steady pace. Eddy still held his rifle. She didn't see the dark-haired man.

Her heart squeezed tight. Growing up and in her line of work, she'd stared down a grizzly bear and an angry moose. But the terror that invaded every molecule of her body right now was more intense than anything she'd ever experienced. Fear threatened to paralyze her. She couldn't take a deep breath or think of what their next move should be.

They'd be spotted as soon as they left the cover of the juniper tree.

Jesse glanced one way and then the other, then looked up toward the mountain peak. He grabbed her hand and squeezed it. "Let's go for it." He locked her in his gaze for a moment.

She saw courage in those brown eyes. He gave her a half nod and then patted her shoulder as if to say "you can do this."

He burst to his feet. She did the same. He ran in a zigzag pattern, making his way toward a rock outcropping that might provide a degree of protection.

Abby pumped her legs as her lungs filled with air.

It took several minutes before the first rifle shot shattered the mountain silence. Judging from the sound, the bullet had come from pretty close to her left.

Inwardly she cringed, but she kept running, pushing up the mountain.

The sound of a bullet propelled out of the barrel of a rifle and moving through space, which she had heard a thousand times in her life, sent an unfamiliar wave of terror through her. She had never been shot at. She had never been the prey. She had been with her brothers when they went hunting and had witnessed the terror an animal felt when it thought it would die. A deer wounded by a bullet, normally a passive animal, would charge you to save its life.

Now she understood what it meant to battle against a death that seemed imminent. How intensely she felt the need to survive, to stay alive.

She lifted her head as she headed up the mountain. She could see the peak, twenty steep yards above her.

Jesse maneuvered so he was between her and Eddy. Was he doing that to protect her from the incoming bullets?

Another shot zinged through the air.

She kept running, praying that the bullets would not find their target. Once they were down on the other side of the mountain, they'd have a measure of safety until Eddy got to the top of the peak.

When she glanced over her shoulder, Eddy and the blond man were closing the distance between them. Both men seemed to be in good shape and weren't tiring at all.

The peak drew closer. They might make it after all. She willed herself to run even faster.

She darted out, separating from Jesse as she scrambled up the mountainside.

Another shot broke the silence around them. This one seemed to have gone wild.

She reached the peak. Jesse was right at her heels.

"There." He pointed down at the other side of the

peak, at the tree line where the forest butted up against a flat meadow.

She wasn't sure what he was indicating. She didn't see anything that looked like an airplane. They made their way down the mountainside and sprinted across the meadow. As they got closer, she saw now that there was a small plane camouflaged by evergreen branches.

Jesse arrived at the airplane first. He pulled away enough branches to open the cockpit door. She continued to yank away the branches to allow visibility through the front windshield. The plane was a small bush model designed to land in less-than-perfect conditions and terrain.

Movement at the top of the mountain peak drew her attention. Eddy had made it to the top and was lining up another shot, while the blond man jogged down the mountain toward them.

Jesse climbed into the plane.

She ripped away several more branches before yanking open the copilot door and slipping into the seat.

Jesse had flipped several switches. Lights on the control panel blinked on, but she did not hear the rumble and whir of an engine firing up.

Abigail was out of breath from running so hard. "Do you know what you're doing?"

Jesse continued to flip switches on the control panel. "I have a pilot's license. This thing hasn't been fired up for a long time. It's gonna take a minute."

Through the windshield, she could see that the blond man had made it to the base of the mountain and was now running across the meadow. He'd have to get within feet of them to make a shot with a handgun count. Eddy, who was halfway down the mountain, lifted the rifle and peered through the scope.

Her heartbeat drummed in her ears and she gripped the armrest a little tighter.

The engine roared to life and Jesse taxied forward. The plane wobbled a bit on the uneven ground.

Eddy gave up on making the shot from where he was perched and jogged toward a rock, where he propped his rifle to steady it.

The blond man was less than ten yards from them.

Jesse pulled a handgun from inside his jacket. "You know how to shoot, right?"

"Of course." Perhaps it was the severe tension of the moment, but she almost laughed out loud. "My dad taught me."

He handed her the gun. "Pretty Boy is coming up on your side."

"Is that what you call him?" She looked again to see that the blond man, Pretty Boy, had drawn even closer. As the plane gained speed, Pretty Boy took aim at her window. The plane bumped along. She opened the co-pilot door and fired off a shot that sent Pretty Boy to the ground. He got right back up. He must not have been hit.

The plane lifted off. When they were about forty feet off the ground, they flew right over Eddy, who was scrambling to line up a shot.

The plane was slow in gaining altitude. Jesse eased the throttle on the pedestal. When she peered out the front windshield, it looked like they wouldn't clear the tops of the trees.

Jesse stared straight ahead. "Come on, baby. You can do this for me."

As they flew over the tops of trees, she thought she heard branches brushing the underside of the airplane.

Abby let up on the death grip she had on the armrest of the seat and released the breath she didn't realize she'd been holding. "We made it."

He turned to her. She liked the way a spark came into his brown eyes when he smiled. "Yes, we made it."

She unclicked her seat belt and turned around to see what kind of cargo was in the plane. A tarp had come off what looked like neatly stacked rectangles of something. She leaned over the seat to get a better look.

Jesse's face blanched. "It's not what you think."

Her breath caught in her throat. The tarp had been covering what looked like bricks of some kind of drug. A mixture of fear and anger swirled through her. "And what am I supposed to think?" Men couldn't be trusted on any level. She was in an airplane with a criminal.

"Abigail, I can explain," he said.

She slammed a hand on her hip. "I just bet you can explain." All the anger she felt over Brent's betrayal flooded back through her. What Jesse had done was even worse. Why was this happening? Did she have a sign on her forehead that said she was okay with being deceived by men?

The plane began to wobble.

"Face forward in your seat, put your seat belt on." Jesse said in a raised voice.

One wing dropped lower than the other. She secured herself in the seat. "What's wrong with the plane?"

Jesse clicked some switches on the instrument panel. "Either we're having engine trouble or Eddy was able to hit the plane, and we just didn't hear it over the sound of the motor." He stared through the windshield. "Either way, I'm going to have to crash-land this baby."

Abigail's heart seized with terror as she stared through the windshield, watching the treetops grow ever closer.

Jesse stared out at the ground below as the plane lost altitude. He searched the landscape for a flat spot that could serve as a landing strip. What he saw was mostly forest and mountains.

"You know this area. Is there any place close by that would be flat enough to land on?"

Abigail stared through the front windshield. It took her a moment to respond. "Everything looks different from up here. Veer off to the west. I think there's a grassy patch on the other side of that cluster of trees." Her voice trembled as she spoke, a sign that revealed the level of fear she was battling.

The plane continued to sputter and lurch up and down as though traveling on waves. Jesse changed course. He dropped altitude as they drew near to the trees. He could see the flat spot Abigail had referred to. When he checked the gauges, he saw that they had lost substantial fuel since takeoff. The gas tank might have been hit. But some other damage was making it hard to keep the wings level.

The plane drew even closer to the ground, skimming the treetops. The strip of land was not very long. He'd be pushing it to try to get the plane stopped before they ran into the trees on the other side.

He nose-dived the plane, then leveled it off and dropped the landing gear. The wheels touched the ground, and the plane bumped along. The landing was so rough his body felt like he was being shaken from the inside and the outside at the same time.

The aircraft remained on the ground, but continued to rumble toward the trees. The entire cockpit vibrated as the trees drew closer. The nose of the plane shot through them. They rolled along, cutting through the trees that were far apart. Branches snapped until the larger trees served as a sort of net that stopped them. The body of the plane thundered and shook.

Both of them sat, clinging to their chairs while the dust settled, and the plane stopped creaking and groaning.

"If there's a fuel leak, there could be a fire," Jesse said. "You need to get out." He had to find that hard drive, or all of this would be in vain. Lee had died before he could tell Jesse where in the plane he'd hidden it.

Abigail leaned to push on her door. "My door won't open. There's a tree in the way." Her voice was filled with anguish. She slumped back in her seat and stared at the ceiling. Her lower lip quivered.

Jesse reached over and stroked her shoulder. "It's all right. We're on the ground now." He tried to sound reassuring, but they were far from being, literally or figuratively, out of the woods. He stood up from his seat and took a step toward the cargo area. "You can get out from my side."

"And what are you going to do?"

Her accusatory tone got under his skin. He was an honest man. "There's something I need to locate."

"You said yourself this plane could catch on fire."

He had no time to argue with her. "I'll explain later. Get outside and tell me if you can assess why we went down." He didn't mean to sound harsh, but time was of the essence.

She scowled but shifted over to his seat and pushed open the door.

Jesse scanned the cargo area. He flung open several storage drawers, not finding anything that looked like a hard drive. Maybe Lee had taped it underneath the control panel. He hurried toward the nose of the plane and ran his hands underneath the control panel. Nothing. He flung open a storage box behind the copilot seat and rifled through the contents. Not there.

The pilot-side door screeched open and Abigail stuck her head in. "There are flames shooting out."

He stopped his mad search long enough to register what she had said. A thunderous noise that sounded as though it was contained within a bubble surrounded him. A small explosion from the fire. More, bigger explosions might follow.

He needed to find that hard drive.

Smoke filled the interior of the plane. He coughed. His vision blurred.

He felt Abigail grab his hand and drag him out of the plane.

When his vision cleared, he saw a wall of flames by the plane's engine. Smoke began to rise in the air. He coughed, feeling a sense of defeat.

He hadn't found the hard drive. The cartel would be set on revenge even more because of their loss of product. He wasn't sure they had fired shots at the airplane. It didn't seem like they would risk the drugs burning up, but then again, if he got away in the plane they'd lose the drugs for sure and he could identify the three men.

Abigail rose to her feet. "It looks like it's too wet

for the trees to catch on fire. The fact that it's been a wet spring will keep the fire from spreading." She still sounded shaken and upset.

Already the fire was dying down. That single burst of flame must have consumed all the oxygen and fuel. Part of the plane would still be intact when the flames died down, though the interior had filled with smoke.

Smoke rose up in the air. Probably not enough to be noticed by anyone in Fort Madison, the little town they'd hiked in from. The three men who had been after them would see it and know where they were located. They hadn't flown that far before landing.

Still trying to clear his mind, he placed his hands on his hips. What now? They needed to get off this mountain before the thugs found them. "Can you guide me back down to Fort Madison?"

She crossed her arms and glared at him, then angled her body so she had a view of the smoldering plane.

"Look, I understand your suspicions, and I'm sorry I wasn't up-front with you." The less she knew the better, for her own safety. "I'm a drug enforcement agent. I was set up by another agent so it looks like I was working with drug dealers. I needed to get this plane back. It has evidence that could clear me."

"And you came up here all by yourself? Don't you people usually work as a team? Even if you are a DEA agent, I'm sure they end up on the wrong side of the law all the time."

Without the evidence, he had no idea who in the home office would even believe that he'd been framed. As far as the agency was concerned, he'd gone rogue. Though DEA work involved a level of deception with undercover work, he knew it was for the cause of justice.

He was a man who always tried to do the right thing. It bothered him that his character had been so smeared by Lee's frame-up. The only thing that bothered him more right now was the way Abigail was looking at him with suspicion.

"Look, we both need to get out of here and back to civilization as fast as possible." He took a step toward her.

Her mouth twitched, and she narrowed her eyes at him.

"Please trust me. I'm one of the good guys."

"*Trust* you?" The word seemed to upset her, when he had hoped that it would build a bridge between them.

"Abigail, what are you going to do? Those men are armed and they still have gear and food."

Again, she studied him for a long moment, probably considering her options.

He took a step toward her. "I need your expertise to get out of these mountains as fast as possible, and you need my protection in case those guys do catch up with us."

She stared at him, her mouth drawn into a tight line. "I wish I had my backpack." She turned sideways in the direction from which they had come.

He let out a breath. At least now she seemed to be in problem-solving mode. Maybe she was starting to come around, regardless of what she might think of him. "Going back for your gear is not an option. The fire is dying out in that plane. I'll go back in there and see if there's anything we can use."

A raindrop hit his nose. Good for drowning the fire, not so good for staying dry.

Abigail jogged toward the forest. "We can stay drier in the trees."

He liked the use of the word *we*. She seemed to understand the need for them to stay together. Really, he needed her more than she needed him. She was an experienced guide. She probably knew how to defend herself against man and animal. He was a city boy and could not navigate his way out of a paper bag in an environment like this.

By the time he reached the edge of the forest, the drizzle had turned into a downpour. The fire would be put out that much faster. Unless other people were close by, the chance of the smoke alerting someone other than the criminals that a plane had crash-landed was close to zero. The fire hadn't burned long enough and the smoke hadn't risen high enough for it to be seen in town.

It was possible that there were other hikers in these mountains who might alert authorities once they returned to Fort Madison. But Fort Madison was a three-day hike away. Help from the outside was not something they could count on.

Abigail found shelter underneath the long branches of an older evergreen. She crouched down and pulled her knees toward her chest. He sat down beside her. The rain pelted against the higher branches, but he and Abigail remained relatively dry.

"We need to assess what we have to work with. I have a Swiss Army knife I always carry with me, an energy bar in my jacket pocket and waterproof matches," Abigail said matter-of-factly.

He liked that she was thinking about how they were going to get off this mountain. "I have a gun with eight bullets left in it." He rifled through the pockets of his jacket. "And a metro pass, a very old piece of hard candy, a couple of paper clips, a pocket Bible and a tire gauge I forgot to put back in my toolbox the last time I checked my tire pressure."

She tilted her head and raised her eyebrows. "That is not very helpful. Even MacGyver would say that's not much to work with."

He laughed. "You watch that show, too?"

The faintest hint of a smile, a spasm almost, lit up Abigail's face. "I might have caught a rerun a time or two. That show's been around forever."

He liked her smile, however brief it had been.

Her expression turned serious once again, eyebrows drawn close together. "You didn't follow my instructions. When I told you how to pack, I said there were some essential things you needed to have on your person at all times."

"I know. I didn't think I'd be hiking out," he said.

"Rule number one about being in the mountains— you always hope for the best but plan for the worst."

"Yes, I remember you said that." He leaned a little closer to her. "Sorry I'm such a bad student."

She pulled away. She was still a little prickly. Maybe her coldness was about something more than just him.

"By landing where we did, we have gotten quite a ways from the main trail, which is the most direct route back into town," she said.

"But you can get us back into Fort Madison?"

She rolled her eyes. "Of course I can. It's what I do for a living."

"We can't wait here much longer. Hopefully, that fire will die out."

He listened for a moment to the rain falling on the higher branches, creating a sort of melody.

"Yes, I suppose we need to get moving as quickly as possible."

He imagined that she was thinking the same thing he was. Though they had a head start on the three men, waiting for the plane to stop burning would cost them valuable time, but hiking with no supplies could be costly, too. It was just a matter of time before the men tracked them to this spot.

THREE

With the rain still falling, Abigail ventured out of the trees to look at the plane wreckage. She was grateful for the baseball hat she wore and the waterproof jacket. Though it was spring, the mountain temperatures could still dip into the teens. She had dressed in layers. She was grateful to be warm and mostly dry.

Jesse followed behind her as they stepped out into the open. The plane was smoldering, and the stench of smoke and melting plastic was still heavy in the air. Her eyes watered.

She removed the bandanna from around her neck and placed it over her mouth.

Jesse coughed. "You think of everything, don't you?"

"It's called being prepared." There was a slight edge to her voice that caught her by surprise. Searching a drug plane for something that might help them survive with a man who might be a criminal was not her idea of a good time. "Sorry, I didn't mean to sound snippy."

"It's all right." He touched her shoulder. "I should have listened better when you gave me instructions before we left town for this trek."

Again, that stab to her heart sent waves of anger and

sadness through her. Brent had destroyed her ability to trust her own judgment. She had no idea if Jesse was being honest with her or not about being framed. He seemed apologetic and almost…nice. She clenched her jaw. *Nothing is as it appears.*

She was certain of only one thing—they needed to work as a team if they were going to get back to town. When she stepped into the plane, the toxic smell of burnt plastic was even stronger.

Jesse drew up his jacket collar over his nose and mouth. "Whoa, we better get this over with as quickly as possible. I'm sure breathing this stuff isn't good for our lungs. I'll look toward the back. You search the front."

She opened a box behind the copilot's seat and the storage pouches beside each of the seats. After searching for several minutes, she came up with a water bottle, several packages of candy and a hat. She tossed the hat toward Jesse. "Put that on. It will help keep the rain and sun out. What did you come up with?"

He caught the hat and placed it on his head. He pointed at the tarp that covered the drugs. "We could use that for shelter if we had to."

The drugs looked like they had been only partially damaged. The fire had consumed some of the plastic the bricks were packaged in. She shivered but not from the cold. How had she gotten connected to drugs and drug dealers? She had lived a really sheltered life and hadn't even rebelled as a teenager like her brothers had. All of this was so out of her frame of reference. Maybe if she hadn't been so naive, she would have realized what a player Brent was. And maybe she wouldn't be in this mess with Jesse. "Yes," she said, "bring the tarp."

She grabbed a lined jacket that was hanging over the back of the copilot seat. She could fashion a makeshift backpack out of it.

"Also, I found this." He held up an unopened energy drink and a bowie knife. He put the energy drink in his pocket and zipped it shut.

The knife gave her the shivers all over again. "Let's get out of here." She pushed open the pilot's door and jumped out.

Jesse didn't follow her. He must have still been searching for something—what, she didn't know. A cold wave of fear washed over her. Was he looking for drug money?

She tilted her head toward the sky. Dark clouds all around, no sign of blue sky. The storm was probably going to last awhile.

Abigail retreated toward the trees. She pulled out her Swiss Army knife and slit the lining of the jacket she'd grabbed at the bottom hem. She cut holes at the ends of the sleeves and in the shoulders.

Jesse finally joined her.

"Find what you were looking for?"

"No," he said.

So, he wasn't going to be forthcoming about what he was searching for. "Turns out those paper clips you had in your pocket might come in handy."

He dug through his pockets. "Well, what do you know." He handed them to her. His fingers brushed over her palm. "Maybe I'll earn my MacGyver certificate after all."

She straightened the paper clips and then drew them through the holes she'd cut in the jacket, so the ends of the sleeves were attached to the shoulders. She put the candy and the water bottle in the backpack she'd just made. "Toss that knife in here, too."

Admiration spread across his face. "Wow, I'm impressed." He stepped toward her and placed the knife and drink in her pack. "What about the tarp?"

She handed him her knife. "Cut a hole in it and use it for a rain poncho. This storm is going to last for a bit."

As if to confirm her prediction, lightning flashed in the sky, followed by thunder a few seconds later.

He slit an opening into the center of the tarp. "What about you? Won't you get wet?"

She was touched by his concern for her. "My coat is waterproof."

"We better get moving." A wave of fear passed through her. "Those other men will catch up with us sooner or later, right?"

He nodded and tipped the brim of his hat to her.

They stepped out of the forest into the downpour. Abigail assessed where they were based on the mountain peaks. She didn't doubt her ability to get them back on the trail, but it would take some doing. She wasn't familiar with this part of the forest, but she knew if they moved in the general direction of the mountain peak referred to as Angel's Peak, they would intersect with the trail. When they got closer and the immediate landscape became familiar, she would pinpoint the trail's location with more accuracy and then figure out the best way to avoid the men. Maybe by staying close to the trail but not on it.

For now, all they had to do was keep Angel's Peak in front of them.

They stepped out into the downpour, hiked across

the wide-open strip of land where the plane had gone down and entered the forest on the other side.

They walked side by side without speaking, their footsteps pounding out a rhythm. Fear and doubt played at the corners of her mind. Heading back to the trail was the quickest way to get back to town, but it was also the most obvious. Those three men had followed her and Jesse up the mountain without being spotted, so it was clear they had some tracking skills and were in good shape.

In her mind, she saw the different topographical maps she'd studied of the various areas she'd camped and all the places she'd taken clients in these mountains over the few months she'd worked for Big Sky Outfitters. She still wasn't sure what the best strategy for avoiding the men was. Trying to come up with a less obvious way down the mountain could get them lost. They did not have the food or gear for that.

The forest thinned as the rain pelted her hat and drizzled from the trees. They stepped out into a flat area, where it looked like a forest fire had passed through. The grass had not grown back in yet. The ground was muddy, causing her hiking boots to make a suctioning sound with every step.

Jesse slid, his legs going into a split before he righted himself. "Kind of slippery out here."

"Yes, watch your step."

They trudged on through the slick mud. Jesse's tarp poncho made swishing noises as he moved. The rain tapped out a rhythm.

He did a double step to catch up with her. "Look, I'm an extrovert. This silence is killing me."

He'd been plenty talkative on his way up here, mostly

about the sports he played and music he liked. Nothing in his conversation had hinted that he was in law enforcement.

She had spent most of her time trying to teach him how to read the landscape. Since she had thought he would be hiking out alone, she'd tried to explain possible scenarios he might encounter and what to do.

She didn't really see the point of getting to know him better. "I'm an introvert. I like the silence."

"Suit yourself." He shrugged and kept pace with her. A moment later, he started to hum what sounded like the annoying theme song from a children's program her niece watched.

"Okay," she said. "You win. If it will stop you from humming that song, we can talk."

He smiled. "Good." He glanced over his shoulder. His smile turned grim and his voice dropped half an octave. "Never mind."

She spun around. Behind them, at the other end of the muddy field, two of their three pursuers barreled toward them.

Jesse scanned the landscape around them.

Nowhere to run. Nowhere to hide.

They were out in the open, exposed. Some rocks at the edge of the field looked to be their only option.

"Get over there as fast as you can," he said, directing Abigail toward the rocks.

The mud bogged them down. And now the hillside slanted up.

Abigail glanced over her shoulder. "Those trees are closer. It's easier to go across than up in this sticky gumbo." Abigail had already redirected her steps.

Where the wilderness was concerned, he'd trust her choices over his. He slipped a few paces behind her. "We shouldn't bunch together." Better to have two targets than one.

Abigail jogged through the mud in a sure-footed way. He stumbled behind, running in a zigzag pattern so it would be harder to shoot him. The tarp he wore as a rain poncho slowed him down.

The men had changed course, as well. Eddy had stopped to line up a shot, while Pretty Boy sprinted toward them. He wondered what had become of the third man, the one with the dark, slicked-back hair. Cell phones didn't work in the high mountains. But what if the men had some other way to communicate to bring in even more men to the hunt?

The special phone Abigail had given him in case he got lost on his way down was in his backpack. Lost forever, or maybe the men had found it and used it.

Abigail drew nearer to the trees.

The percussive bang of the rifle shot leaving the barrel of the gun pummeled his eardrums, but he did not hear the bullet hit, which meant it must have sunk into the mud. Abigail disappeared into the trees with a backward glance at him. His feet felt weighted down by the amount of mud on them. He lifted his legs, pumping fast and hard even as the mud suctioned around his boots. Pretty Boy had closed the distance between them and Eddy had run a dozen yards in order to line up another shot.

The trees were ten yards away. He saw no sign of Abigail—she must have kept running. He sprinted, fixing his gaze on the edge of the forest. The trees grew larger in his field of vision. Another bullet from the rifle traveled through the air. This one split the bark of the tree inches in front of him just as he entered the forest.

His heart beat a little faster, knowing how close he'd come to taking a bullet. A vibrating branch indicated the direction in which Abigail had run. There was no trail to follow in this part of the forest. The ground cover of pine needles, leaves and broken branches was thick. Some of the mud came off his boots, but he still felt like he was running with weights on his feet.

He caught sight of Abigail's blond braid flying as she ran. He hurried to catch up with her. He could hear the thugs yelling at each other as they entered the forest.

Abigail traveled steadily uphill. She must have had some kind of plan or route in mind that would throw off the pursuers. As the trees thinned, the terrain grew drier, populated with tiny pebbles and then rocks. He caught up with Abigail.

His words came out between gasping breaths. "Do you know where you're going?"

"Just getting away," she said, out of breath, as well.

Somehow, he'd hoped she had a better plan than haphazardly running away. He spotted some brush up ahead that was tall enough to hide behind. "Keep going," he said. "I'll try to stop them."

He crouched behind the brush, peering out to see if he could spot the two other men. Pretty Boy was the first to emerge from the trees. Eddy was probably slowed down by having to carry the rifle. Pretty Boy glanced in one direction, darted a few paces in the other and then ran up the mountain. Abigail was in plain sight. But she was too far away for Pretty Boy to get a decent shot with just a handgun.

Jesse waited with his gun drawn. Pretty Boy's attention was on Abigail as he ran toward her. At best, Jesse would get one shot before Pretty Boy had time to react. He had to make it count. The blond man continued to fix his gaze on Abigail as she made her way up the mountain.

Eddy emerged from the trees and took the same path as Pretty Boy, though he moved slower, bracing the rifle on his shoulder.

Pretty Boy drew closer to the brush where Jesse was hiding. Jesse waited, gripping his gun and listening to his own heartbeat drumming in his ears. Pretty Boy's footsteps grew louder, more intense. Jesse peered through the brush, which was just starting to leaf out.

He jumped up, located his target and fired off a shot. Knowing that Pretty Boy could just as easily shoot him, he took off running before assessing if he'd hit his target.

He heard a yelp behind him. Either Pretty Boy was injured or angry or both.

Abigail had reached the top of the hill and disappeared over the other side. Jesse willed his legs to move faster. His ears detected another rifle shot just as he edged toward the top of the hill. His heart pounded from the effort of running uphill and from the threat of death that pressed ever closer.

The other side of the hill was a boulder field that led to a river bottom, and beyond that a forest. He caught up with Abigail just as another rifle shot shattered the silence around them. The men had made it to the top of the hill. He grabbed her sleeve and pulled her toward a larger rock.

Both of them gasped for air, taking only a moment to rest before running again. He could hear the men's footfalls on the rocks as they closed in. Abigail headed toward the river. He couldn't see a bridge anywhere.

She approached the river's edge, glanced over her shoulder as the two men gained on them, then turned back and dived into the rushing waters. He watched her as she was carried downstream. That didn't seem like much of an escape plan.

What choice did he have? He jumped in, as well. The freezing water shocked his system. He drifted downstream, still stunned by the cold that enveloped him. Behind him he could hear rifle shots.

Abigail dived underwater. The tarp he was using as a rain poncho weighed him down and made it hard to maneuver against the current. He dived underwater and slipped out of it but held on to it as the river carried him farther along.

When he resurfaced, the river had taken him around a bend. He could no longer see the pursuers. Only one of the men had been hauling a smaller backpack. Would they jump in after them or try to find another way across the river?

He watched as Abigail swam toward the opposite shore. As the water grew shallower, she stood up and dragged herself onto the bank, flopping down in the grass on her stomach.

The current pulled him farther downstream as he struggled to get to shore. He grabbed hold of a tree limb that hung over the water and strained to pull himself up the steep embankment. He clawed the ground and reached out to grab onto any vegetation that grew close to the shore.

He shivered, and his body seemed to be vibrating from the exertion of the run and plunge into the cold water. He pushed himself to his feet and headed back upriver, where Abigail had come ashore.

As he moved through the forest, the cold seemed to seep down to the marrow of his bones. It was early evening and springtime, but the water in the mountain stream had been freezing.

Jesse heard Abigail before he saw her. It sounded like she was banging sticks together. When he found her in a clearing, she was gathering logs and twigs. Water dripped off her wet clothes. "We need to get a fire started."

"Was there no other option besides jumping in a freezing river?" His teeth chattered from the cold.

"Yes, there was another option, Jesse—dying from a bullet wound." She glared at him. "I made the best choice I could in a tough situation."

It was the first time she'd used his first name. All the way up the mountain before they had encountered the three men, she'd called him Mr. Santorum.

"I would appreciate some help gathering some tinder." She held up a trembling hand. "I'm freezing, too."

"They might see the smoke rising up." He was still concerned about their safety.

"Or they can find our frozen corpses." Maybe it was just because she was cold and exhausted, but she didn't seem to like being questioned about her decision. Her voice softened. "We'll keep the fire small and build it in an area that can't be seen from far away. A lot of this wood is wet from all the spring rain, but stuff in sheltered areas is likely to be drier." With the handful of sticks she'd gathered, she moved deeper into the trees.

He searched the area, finding some twigs and a couple of smaller logs that seemed pretty dry. He found her in a clearing where the trees created a sort of canopy that shielded the fire from view.

She had gathered moss and a few twigs. She blew on the flickering flames before putting a few bigger twigs on the fire. He sat down beside her as she put some bigger logs on the fire. It smoked a bit from the dampness of the logs.

He laid down the logs he'd found and sat beside her.

The fire began to throw some heat. He put his palms up to it.

She picked up the tarp from where he'd dropped it, then peeled off her coat and the vest underneath. She threw them on a nearby log, where the heat from the fire would dry them out. Then she turned toward him. "Hand me your coat. You'll dry out faster this way."

He took off his coat and tossed it toward her.

Still dripping wet, she perched close to the fire on her knees and crossed her arms over her body. "You know, I've been part of a team that found lost hunters in the most impossible places, and I've guided people to safety under extreme weather conditions. No one has ever died or been seriously injured on my watch."

He wasn't sure why she was telling him this. "I can appreciate that."

"I have worked as a guide since I was a teenager. I come from a family of guides. Eighty percent of the people who want to come up to these remote regions are men, and every single time, I have to prove myself and be questioned in a way that I've never seen happen to male guides."

The fire crackled with a rhythm that was harmonious and comforting. As it grew, the heat surrounded him.

He stared at the flames. Now he knew why she was so upset with him. "I'm sorry I questioned your choice."

"I don't have a chip on my shoulder. It's just that it gets old after a while. What I did back there probably kept us alive."

This wasn't even her fight. It was his mess to untangle, and yet she felt a responsibility to get him out of the mountains at the risk of her own life. "I never should have dragged you into all this. It's just that I couldn't get up here on my own. I would have died."

In that moment, he felt how alone he was in the world. Lee had so thoroughly smeared his name that he didn't know if anyone at the DEA would believe his innocence. He'd worked with those men and women for close to seven years, but there was no way to discern who would turn him in and who would rely on what they knew about his character.

She stared at the fire. Her voice grew softer. "Well, whether I like it or not, we are in this together. I can't in good conscience just walk away from you, and I kind of think those men would kill me just as fast as they would kill you, given what I know and what I've seen."

He felt a rush of gratitude toward her. "Thank you, Abigail."

"I will get you off this mountain alive," she said.

He felt a new appreciation for her and how she had taken on such a responsibility in the face of so much danger.

He hated that he'd put her at risk. That had not been his intention. Everything was so tenuous and uncertain. Abigail could identify the men who had come after them. Would she even be safe once they got back to Fort Madison…if they got back to Fort Madison?

FOUR

As she warmed up, Abigail repositioned herself, crossing her legs beneath her. The heat from the fire intensified. She'd stopped shivering at least, though her clothes were still damp. She tore open her makeshift backpack, grateful to see that she hadn't lost anything from her plunge into the river.

She pulled out a candy bar with the wrapper adhered to it from being exposed to the heat. It was now soggy. Once she peeled off the wrapper, she broke the candy bar in half and handed one section to Jesse. "You'll need this to keep up your strength."

She rose to her feet and took the protein bar out of her jacket pocket. She broke that in half as well, offering him a portion. "The carbs from the candy bar will burn off pretty fast. The protein will sustain you."

Jesse studied her with those rich brown eyes. "Thanks." He chewed the protein bar and spoke between bites. "So, what's the plan now?"

She still didn't know what to think of Jesse Santorum. He didn't act like a drug dealer. He seemed almost decent.

It would be nightfall soon. They'd gotten seriously off course by jumping in the river. "Those men will probably track down the river several miles and find the bridge. If they jumped in after us, we should hear them coming in less than an hour. But if they go downriver to the bridge, we have several hours or more before they can pick up our trail."

Jesse wrapped his arms around his chest and scooted a little closer to the fire. "I suppose it would take them a while to figure out where we came to shore, anyway."

"I think the best thing for us to do is to rest and get dry," she said. "We'll head out at twilight."

Jesse pulled his gun from his waistband and sat it on a log. "But sooner if the men show up."

Navigating at night was never easy, but they could follow the river back up to where they'd been. The darkness would shield them from view. She felt a little flutter of fear. "Yes, of course. It's hard to predict what the men will do exactly."

He looked directly at her. "The only sure thing is that they will come after us sooner or later."

His words sent a new surge of terror through her. She took in a breath to clear her mind. "Why don't you try to get some rest? That's what I'm going to do."

She stretched out on the mossy ground, using her arm as a pillow. She closed her eyes and listened to the crackle of the fire. She heard Jesse shuffling around.

"I think one of us should stand watch," he said.

"Or sit watch." She spoke without opening her eyes. "We have a limited food supply. Food is energy. You need to conserve what energy you do have."

"Gotcha," he said, sitting down.

"Go ahead and keep watch for now, but you will need to get some sleep, too." Dragging his sorry, tired self upriver was not her idea of a good time. They both needed all the energy they could muster.

The fog of sleep invaded her brain, and she drifted off into a deep sleep, where she dreamed she was running on a trail pursued by a dark figure. She awoke with a start, bursting into a sitting position.

Jesse sat on the other side of the fire. He must have added wood to it to keep it going. "Bad dreams?"

"Yes, one where I'm running but can't seem to make any progress."

There was something comforting knowing that Jesse was watching and listening for any sign of danger.

She closed her eyes and took in another deep breath. She was accustomed to sleeping on the hard ground. Sleep came easily to her.

When she awoke again, the sky had turned charcoal and the birds had stopped singing. She sat up and stretched. Jesse was still sitting with his back to the log. He must have put his gun back in his waistband.

"Did you sleep at all?"

"I rested my eyes some," he said. "You must have fallen into a deep sleep. You snore a little."

"I don't snore," she said.

He laughed. "Just a little. A very ladylike kind of snore."

She hadn't meant to sound so offended. She appreciated that he was able to see the humor of the moment.

She rose to her feet and slipped into her coat, which was completely dry. "Why don't we have that energy drink you found?" she said.

He pulled it from his pocket, opened it and offered her the first sip. She took several gulps before handing it back to him.

"I already folded the tarp and put it in the pack. I'll carry it for a while. Lead the way," he said.

They stepped out into the evening light. She wove through the trees, following the sound of the rushing river. "They must be tracking us up from the bridge or they would have been on our tail by now."

"How would they know there was a bridge down-river? They don't know this country like you do," he said.

"There are maps of the area. I'm sure they had one to follow us up here and not be noticed. And if you walk beside a river long enough, you usually come to a bridge. To stay on us the way they did, we have to assume that at least one of them has some tracking skills."

"Yes," he said, coming alongside her.

Though it was hard to see in the dim light, she picked the path that was more level to walk on.

"Are we going back to where we got derailed?"

"It's the easiest way to navigate back to the trail," she said.

"They could be watching, waiting for us to return."

Once again, it felt like he was questioning her judgment. "Do you have a better plan? I said I would get you back to the trail and down the mountain."

His response was gentle. "I trust your expertise, Abigail. I don't know what their next move will be. That's what I'm worried about. The only thing we can assume is that they are still looking for us."

Something inside her softened when he didn't respond in a hostile way to her oversensitivity. Her reaction wasn't about Jesse; it was about Brent. Her anger at Brent simmered just beneath the surface and she'd projected it onto Jesse. His betrayal had caused her whole life to be turned inside out. Every assumption she'd made was no longer true. Since their engagement, every plan she'd made had revolved around thinking she and Brent would be married. The truth was, once she got down this mountain, she didn't know what her life would look like anymore.

They came out into the open, where a large sand-bar bordered the river. On the other side of the shore, the deer had come to the river's edge to drink. They lifted their heads and stared with curiosity at Abigail and Jesse.

In the distance, the sun sank low on the horizon and then slipped behind a mountain peak. She hiked, letting the sound of the river determine their path, even when they had to slip back into the trees or thick brush. She took the lead as they walked in silence. The landscape became more shadow and outlined as night fell.

Jesse was probably right about one of the men watching the trail where it intersected with the place they had been headed. The three men could split up, each searching a different area. She had no idea if they had walkie-talkies or a way of communicating. They could just as easily have searched Jesse's backpack and taken the satellite phone. "I wonder what happened to the dark-haired guy? Why wasn't he with those other two?"

Jesse took a moment to answer, probably jolted from whatever he'd been thinking about in the long silence. She listened to his feet pad on the ground behind her. "I don't know. Maybe he stayed with the plane. Some part of that product might be salvageable, but they've got to figure out a way to get it out."

"There are only two ways to get this high up the mountain. On foot and by air." She tilted her head toward the sky, half expecting to see another bush plane.

Certainly, they wouldn't be able to mobilize that fast. That satellite phone would be the only thing that would allow them to communicate with anyone not on the mountain.

When it got darker, they slowed their pace. Abigail stopped to fill her bottle with water from the river. They both drank several gulps. She refilled it and they continued on through the darkness. Stars sprinkled across the night sky, and the temperature dropped several degrees.

The forest opened up. They walked out onto a wide sandbar. Across the rushing river, partway up the mountain, a light flashed.

Jesse stopped and stared out across the river. The light blinked in and out as it moved down the mountain. "I suppose there are other people up here. Hikers and such."

"Some," said Abigail. "Most people would have set up camp for the night by now, though. They wouldn't be on the move like this."

The night breeze seemed to carry even more of a chill with it. She struggled to take in a deep breath. As she watched the light blink in and out of visibility, she was pretty sure at least one of their pursuers was making his way down the mountain toward the river.

As they traversed along the river, Jesse wrestled with all the unknowns. Would the men meet them on the trail? Would they track them by crossing the river and coming at them from behind? The only thing he was sure of was that the men would not just give up and head down the mountain.

As the sandbar narrowed, Abigail guided him back into the trees.

The silence made him crazy. It was too much of an opportunity for his thoughts to send him in a direction that messed with his composure. The whole trip up here was, at this point, an act of futility. The plane was still stuck in the trees, was probably not flyable, and he had no idea where the hard drive that would prove his innocence was.

His thoughts raced faster than a hamster on a wheel. Was all of this for nothing? And now he had gotten Abigail involved. He had to talk or his negative thoughts would derail him into a place of despair. "So did you always want to be a guide?"

She walked for several paces before answering. "It was sort of inevitable. My whole family is into hiking, camping and fishing, anything to do with the outdoors."

"Ever want to do anything else?" He stumbled over something in the dark.

She whirled around to face him, reaching out for his arm. "You all right?"

"It's getting hard to see."

"Test your step before you take it by putting your toe down first," she said.

The forest opened up, and they had a view of the river and the mountain on the other side. The light was still blinking in and out of view, moving ever closer to the river. Abigail slowed her step. He sensed her fear.

He tried to lighten the moment by returning to his question. "If you did something other than be a wilderness guide, what would it be?"

"My turn," she said. "You already asked me a question."

"Fair enough." He was glad she had decided to play along. The conversation served as a distraction from speculating when the three men would catch up with them. "Ask away."

"Did you always want to be a DEA agent?"

"No, I was a pretty good musician in college, but you know how that goes."

"I never would have guessed that. What instrument did you play?"

"Guitar—" Something rustled in the brush and both of them fell silent. He stepped a little closer to her. She pulled him back toward a tree with a wide trunk. She tugged on his elbow, indicating they needed to crouch down.

Then he saw the flash of a light and heard footsteps.

His heartbeat revved up ten notches.

It appeared the men had tracked them by crossing the bridge and coming up behind them. Maybe the light they saw coming toward the river was one of the other men, or someone not connected to them at all.

No voices. No exchange of instructions. Maybe it was just one man after them. The fire they'd built would be a clear indication of where they'd been.

The footsteps drew closer. This wasn't much of a hiding place. If the man shone the flashlight in this direction, they'd be spotted.

Abigail tapped his arm. She was already moving, probably toward a better hiding place. He could barely make out her silhouette; she was a shadow among shadows. She moved so quietly, he couldn't hear her. He had to guess at where she was going. He reached out a hand, touching the fabric of her coat.

She tugged on his sleeve again. He moved closer to her. In the darkness, he touched the roughness of a log and then the silky smoothness of her hair right before she slipped down low. He patted the log to get a feel for it before crawling over it.

Behind them, the flashlight spanned an area like a searchlight moving back and forth. He sank down even more behind the log. He could hear Abigail's gentle breathing. Their heads were close together. Pine needles on the forest floor poked his hand where it rested.

In the darkness, his heartbeat drummed in his ears.

The light swept over the top of the log.

Though slow and soft, the footsteps became more distinct. A boot broke some twigs on the ground. It sounded like the man was less than five feet away from them.

Somewhere in the distance, an owl hooted.

Jesse held his breath, waiting for the footsteps to resume. He counted the seconds. Silence.

Then he heard the sound of the man letting out a breath. Why wasn't he moving on? The man took a step and swept the light over the area around the log once again.

Jesse remained as still as a statue.

More footsteps and then silence.

A second before the light landed on their faces, Abigail sprang to her feet. Jesse jumped up, as well.

She was running through the trees. Branches creaked where she had pushed them out of the way. He followed the sound of her footsteps, stumbling in the darkness. Behind them, the light bobbed up and down, headed directly toward them.

The footsteps were loud and intensified as the pursuer drew closer, like the drumbeat before a firing squad.

Though he could only make out moving shadows

and vague outlines, Jesse homed in on the noises that Abigail made as she retreated deeper into the forest. He felt as though he was a blind man running, and reached out his arms to feel when low-hanging branches were in front of him. One tree branch conked him in the head. He stopped for a moment to get his bearings. He'd lost track of Abigail in the dark.

The man with the flashlight remained close behind, but was unable to close the distance between them.

He took off running, guessing at where Abigail might have gone. She was much more sure-footed and certain of herself in the dark than he was. Suddenly, her hand touched his back at the shoulder.

"This way," she whispered, tugging his jacket at the elbow. She had to have doubled back to find him. He sprinted, staying right at her heels so as not to lose her again.

Footsteps of the pursuer approached at a rapid pace. He wasn't putting any effort into being quiet.

Jesse glanced over his shoulder. The bright light nearly blinded him.

He followed Abigail deeper into the forest and then up a wooded hillside. The hill grew steeper and the climb was more treacherous.

Abigail stopped and climbed up on a big, flat boulder. She held out a hand and helped him onto the rock.

"There." She pointed down the hill, where the flashlight of the pursuer could be seen as he ran parallel to where they'd gone. "People always take the path of least resistance. He'll figure out soon enough that we ditched him and backtrack." She rose to her feet. "But we'll be long gone by then."

Jesse barely had time to catch his breath. He pushed

himself to his feet and fell in beside Abigail. They moved at a slower pace, pushing on through until morning light bathed the mountains and trees with a warm glow that was the color of marmalade.

They stopped to have some gulps of water and eat a handful of candy. They were at a high spot, where Jesse could see most of the landscape below. He saw the trail that disappeared into the mountains. Though he could no longer see the downed airplane, he recognized the grove of trees with the mountain peak behind it. The plane was on the other side of the trees. That was where they had seen the first light coming down the mountain toward the river.

"We've got to get some protein in us." Abigail placed her hands on her hips and turned from side to side. "Critters will be coming out to eat. I'll see if I can trap one. You rest."

She disappeared into the trees. He slumped down, using a tree trunk as a back rest. He closed his eyes and slept until he heard the sound of her footsteps.

"Nothing?"

"There's not a fast-food joint in there." She pointed back at the trees. She sat down beside him. "It takes a while to trap an animal. Let's rest, and I'll check the trap in a few."

Using her hands as a pillow, Abigail rested on her side and drew her legs up toward her chest. He was beginning to think her ability to fall asleep so fast in any condition was a real talent.

He closed his eyes, keeping his ears tuned to the noises around him. He slipped into a deeper sleep. Suddenly his head jerked. An out-of-place clanging reached his ears. It took him a moment to discern if the mechanical noise was part of his dreams or real.

His eyes shot open.

Abigail was still curled up, asleep.

The noise was not part of his dreams. Though he could not see it, he heard a helicopter.

He shook Abigail awake. "Would someone be coming to rescue us in a helicopter?"

She sat up. "No, it takes three days to hike in and three to hike out. No one would be alarmed until either day six or I send out a call for help, which I can't do without the satellite phone. Why?"

"Listen," he said.

The sound of the helicopter had faded.

"I don't hear anything," she said.

"I heard a helicopter." Above him, branches creaked. A crow cawed in the distance. He hadn't imagined it.

Abigail rose to her feet. "I don't hear anything. I'm going to check the trap." She took three steps and then paused, tilting her head toward the empty sky as all the color drained from her face. "Okay, now I hear it, too."

They gazed down the hillside to an open area where a chopper had landed. Jesse peered out from behind a tree, squinting to see better. The dark-haired man they'd seen earlier got out of the chopper, followed by another man, holding the leashes of three bloodhounds.

Abigail's voice was barely above a whisper. "They brought in dogs to hunt us down."

FIVE

Abigail's throat grew so tight it felt like someone was squeezing her neck. Her heart pounded as she watched the dark-haired man get out of the helicopter. "They must have found our backpacks. Our scent will be all over them." A fourth man, a man she hadn't seen before, held the leashes of three tracking dogs.

The helicopter lifted off as soon as the men got out. She recognized the logo on the helicopter. It was from a local business that transported hunters and hikers to the high mountains. No doubt the pilot had no idea what these men were up to. He'd probably been fed some story about what they needed the hounds for.

Jesse tugged on her sleeve. "We better get out of here."

There was not time to check the trap she'd set. She could hear the dogs baying in the distance, getting excited. The dark-haired man spoke into a walkie-talkie. They still had no idea where the two other men were. But the men were clearly in communication with each other.

She took in a breath. "We can't go back to the trail. It will be too easy to track us."

"What do you suggest?"

The dogs continued to bark as they worked their way up the hillside.

Mental pictures of the maps of these mountains flashed through her head again. She started to run up the mountain, still trying to come up with a plan.

The dogs' baying grew louder.

Her mind cleared. She knew what direction they needed to go. Little Spring Creek was not far from where they were. If they ran through it, the dogs would be thrown off the scent.

They sprinted through the trees until she heard the gurgling of the water. The creek was dry most of the year, but with the spring runoff, there would be at least a few inches of water flowing.

The barking of the dogs intensified still. If the pursuers spotted them at the creek, the plan would not work.

Water splashed as she ran through the middle of the creek. Jesse remained close to her. She followed the riverbed as it wound up the mountain. They needed a long-term plan to get off the mountain without being caught. There were other trails that intersected with the trail that led back into town. If they took a circuitous route, they might be able to avoid the dogs. That would take longer, though.

As she ran through the rushing stream, she was grateful for waterproof boots. The bottom of her pant legs were soaked, but her feet remained dry.

The creek curved around some rocks, cutting abruptly to the right. She got out of the water on the opposite side she'd come in on. As they hurried through the forest, her stomach growled. She kept moving until she could no longer hear the dogs.

She collapsed on a large flat rock, trying to catch her breath. "We've burned up a lot of energy. We need to eat."

Jesse took off the makeshift pack and dug into it, pulling out a handful of gummy bears. "Hold out your hand." His knuckles touched her palm as he gave her the candy.

But the carbs would provide only short-term energy. They really needed protein. They ate quickly, washing down the candy with gulps of water, then sprinted again through the trees.

Though farther away, the baying and barking of the dogs reached her ears from time to time. The echo of their persistent noise seemed to invade every crevice of the mountains. She and Jesse were by no means safe from being found.

They jogged for over an hour until they could no longer hear the dogs. Abigail stopped to assess how they could get back on an artery trail that would lead to the main trail. She redirected their steps but grew tired. She stopped and fell to the ground, using a tree trunk as a backrest. Jesse sat down beside her, their shoulders touching.

He rubbed his stomach. "My gut is gurgling."

"Mine, too." Despair came over her. From an early age, she'd been taught how to keep a cool head and solve problems when it came to being in the elements. But this was like nothing she had ever faced before. Doubt plagued the corners of her mind. Could she get them out of here alive?

Jesse leaned a little closer and patted her hand. "We'll figure this out."

His touch warmed her to the bone. She hadn't said

anything. How was it that he was so tuned in to her feelings? She tilted her head and closed her eyes, saying a silent prayer for help and guidance.

When she opened her eyes, Jesse said, "Amen?"

She let out a one-syllable laugh, shaking her head. "How did you know I was praying?"

He offered her a soft smile. "It was a guess. I don't pray much anymore myself."

"Why?"

A shadow seemed to fall across his face. "It's a long story."

She studied him for a moment. For the first time, she noticed that his brown eyes had gold flecks in them. He had a tiny scar on his chin. She wanted to ask him what the story behind the scar was, because most scars came with a story. She wondered why he didn't pray... anymore. She wanted to know more about Jesse.

"We better not stay here long," she said.

Her heart fluttered a little when he nodded and nudged his shoulder against hers.

She sniffed the air. The faint smell of burning wood reached her nose. She rose to her feet. "There's a camp around here somewhere." Using her nose as a guide, she made her way through the trees.

The camp was up the mountain. Chances were, it wasn't one of the men who wanted to kill them. All the same, they needed to exercise caution. Sometime before she'd started working at Big Sky Outfitters, her boss and his now wife had encountered men living up in these mountains planning a bank robbery and other crimes to finance spreading their extreme anti-government beliefs. There might still be some stragglers at this high elevation. Men who were paranoid and prone to violence, choosing to live alone because they couldn't operate in society.

She prayed that wasn't the case. Hopefully, they were just coming upon hikers who liked to camp on the most remote parts of the mountains.

Maybe the light they'd seen coming down the mountain toward the river last night was connected to this camp. That would make more sense than the searchers having gotten so far off the mark in looking for them.

She followed the smell of the fire, choosing her steps carefully so she didn't make any noise. She caught sight of a wisp of smoke rising above the trees. Jesse had pulled his gun from his waistband. He stepped where she stepped.

As they drew nearer, the crackling of the fire reached her ears. She edged a little closer, choosing a tree with a thick trunk to hide behind. Though there were signs that the camp was active, she saw no one other than a raccoon that was gnawing on what looked like a bone. A lean-to that blended with the trees had been formed out of branches and leaves and mud. A metal pot that hung on a small sawhorse-like structure cooked over the fire.

Her stomach growled as the aroma of some sort of soup cooking tickled her nostrils. The occupant of the camp could not have gone far if he'd left his food to cook.

Still holding his gun, Jesse leaned close to her. "Man, I'm starving."

Her mouth watered at the aroma of the soup. "We can't just take the food. We don't know what kind of person we're dealing with here."

"I know. Stealing is wrong," Jesse said. "My stomach

is telling me otherwise, though. Maybe we could eat and leave something as payment."

A further survey of the camp revealed canned goods stacked just inside the lean-to. Whoever lived here must go into town for supplies once in a while or have someone bring them to him.

A breeze caressed Abigail's skin. A tinkling sound reached her ears. The sun reflected off a multifaceted object hanging from a tree. Whoever lived here had fashioned a wind chime from pieces of metal and shiny objects. Seeing it touched something in Abigail's heart. Even in the harshest conditions, people wanted things of beauty to look at. Life could not just be about survival.

A guttural voice sounded behind them. "I think the two of you better turn around real slow."

Abigail swung around to stare into the barrel of a shotgun pointed right at Jesse's heart.

Jesse was unable to tell if the man pointing the shotgun at him was thirty or fifty. Being out in the elements had made his skin leathery. He had a layer of grit on his face that probably wouldn't ever wash off, and his hair, though pulled back in a ponytail, was wild. His beard was also untrimmed and fell to the middle of his chest.

"Drop your gun," said the hermit. His cold blue eyes seemed to pierce right through Jesse.

Jesse obliged. He had to find a way to get his gun back, but now was not the time.

The man pointed the shotgun toward the fire. "Now go on over there, where Lulubell is having her lunch."

Lulubell must be the raccoon. As they approached the fire, the raccoon looked up from the scrap of fatty meat and bone she held in her dexterous paws, but did not run away.

"There's some chairs behind you," the man said as he picked up Jesse's handgun.

Jesse turned a half circle to where he saw a dilapidated lawn chair and a stump. He scooted the chair closer to the fire and offered it to Abigail, keeping one eye on the hermit while he rolled the stump closer to the fire.

The hermit leaned his shotgun against a tree and dropped the backpack he had on the ground. The pack hit the dirt with a thud. Judging from the bulk of it, it was quite full. Of what, Jesse could only guess. Either the man had gone out foraging, or the pack contained supplies he had with him all the time.

Jesse was still not able to get a clear read on the mental stability of the man. Once one of the hermit's hands was free, since he held Jesse's handgun in the other, he rubbed his knuckles on the top of his head repeatedly and did an odd shuffle when he walked—they were mannerisms that suggested mental illness. Then again, a man who spent all his time alone might develop some socially awkward behavior and might be nervous when he did encounter people.

Abigail cleared her throat. "Your soup smells good."

With the handgun still trained on them, the man narrowed his eyes. "Cooks all day to get the flavor just right." Jesse thought he saw a little bit of light come into the man's dull eyes.

"We're real hungry." Her voice held a nervous edge to it. "I'd be willing to trade something for a bowl of that soup."

The man tilted his head slightly and lowered the gun an inch or so. "Whatcha got?"

Abigail never took her eyes off the man. "Show him what we have, Jesse."

Jesse removed the makeshift backpack, pulling out the candy and the knife, and then he emptied the contents of his pockets.

The man licked his lips at the sight of the gummy bears. And then he pointed to Jesse's metro card. "What's that?"

Jesse held it up. The holographic image caught the light. "It's a metro card."

"It's pretty," said the hermit. He walked over to the backpack and unbuckled it, retrieving a leather pouch. "I'll take it and a handful of that candy." He tossed the pouch toward them. "Put the card in there. There are containers inside for soup and the candy." He lifted the gun a little higher, pointing it at Jesse. "You stay put. The girl gets the stuff. No sudden moves."

Abigail rooted through the contents of the lean-to while Jesse placed the card in the pouch, which contained smooth rocks and pieces of metal. She ladled soup for both of them after scooping several handfuls of gummy bears into a container.

With the hermit still watching them, they settled on their chairs. Jesse's spoon had been carved out of wood. The soup, which contained vegetables and some kind of meat, tasted wonderful.

The hermit pointed toward the bowie knife. "I want that, too, but that's a separate trade."

Jesse scraped the last little bit of soup out of the bottom of his bowl, which had been carved from wood, as well.

The hermit sat on the opposite side of the fire. He crossed his legs and rested the gun in the crook of his elbow.

"Your soup is so good." Abigail rubbed her belly and slurped several more spoonfuls.

Though the man's wild beard made it hard to discern his expression, Jesse thought he saw just the faintest of smiles. Abigail seemed to be breaking down his suspicion with her flattery.

"You can have another bowl if you like…on the house," said the hermit.

"Thank you so much." Abigail got up and ladled out more of the hearty soup. She sat back down. "Can my friend have some more?"

The hermit shifted his weight and tilted his head, staring at Jesse. "I'll have to think about that."

Abigail had managed to build some trust with the man, but he still wasn't so sure about Jesse.

The hermit rose to his feet, shuffled across the camp and picked up another log to throw on the fire.

Abigail ate her second bowl of soup at a slower pace than the first. "I'm from Idaho, but my folks used to come out here sometimes to take us camping. I remember when I was a little girl hearing a story about a man who was in a car wreck with his wife. The man, who was driving, survived. The woman didn't. That man disappeared. No one knows what happened to him. The gossip was that he ran up to live in these mountains. Did you ever hear that story?" Abigail had spoken slowly. Compassion saturated each word.

The hermit's eyes clouded with tears. He rose to his feet, running his knuckles over the top of his greasy hair. "I don't know nothing about that."

Abigail had figured out who the man was. Sometimes it wasn't mental illness or paranoia that drove a man to live alone; it was guilt. When he heard the story, Jesse could feel his own heart squeezing tight.

Years ago, he and Melissa had gotten married just out of high school. He had loved her since the seventh grade. Before they could celebrate their first wedding anniversary, Melissa was diagnosed with cancer. She died days after their second anniversary. Though it had been ten years, the pain of the loss, his inability to save the woman he loved, was still as raw as ever.

Jesse saw the hermit with fresh eyes now. They had a great deal in common. Because loving meant risking loss and unbearable pain, he had decided to put his energy into his work and never think about marriage again.

Abigail's spoon scraped the bowl as she finished the last bit of soup. "Jesse, are you okay? You seem kind of faraway."

The fire crackled and the hermit paced. Jesse studied the older man for a moment.

"Just thinking about something that happened a long time ago," he said, surprised by the emotion that rose up in his voice. He cleared his throat. "It's nothing."

In an effort to not fall into the black hole of pain over Melissa, Jesse averted his gaze over to the pack the man had been hauling. Some of the contents had come out when the man had searched for his pouch. Jesse recognized a brick of heroin from the plane, along with some pieces of metal. One of the bricks was broken open, the fine white powder spilling on the ground. Jesse felt a surge of hope. Inside the broken brick was the hard drive he'd been searching for.

In the distance, the baying of the search dogs rose up.

Jesse shot to his feet. "I'm not sure you want to keep that." He tilted his head toward the contents of the backpack. "Men might come for it."

"And they might be willing to trade something for it." The hermit squared his shoulders. "I can handle myself."

The barking of the dogs intensified, indicating they had picked up on a strong scent. Lulubell scurried into the trees. Abigail rose to her feet as well, panic etched across her features.

"I'll trade you the knife for that black thing there." Jesse pointed.

"Deal." The hermit seemed to understand that the dogs meant trouble and that they needed to hurry. He darted over to the backpack and tossed the black box toward Jesse. "You brought those men to my door. Get out of here."

Jesse picked up the knife and handed it to the hermit. There was no time to try to negotiate for the gun. "You might want to hide out for a bit. It's us they're after. We'll lead them away from your camp. But they won't stop at violence to try to get information out of you."

"Don't worry about me." The hermit seemed to understand. He tossed the pack into the lean-to and picked up both guns, shoved the knife into his belt and disappeared into the trees where the raccoon had gone.

It sounded as though the dogs were within a hundred feet of the camp.

"We better get out of here." Abigail bolted toward the edge of the camp, opposite of where the hermit had gone. Jesse shoved the remainder of the gummy bears into the makeshift backpack. He placed the hard drive in the pocket of his coat and hurried after Abigail.

As they pressed on, the hounds' yelping would intensify and then dim and die out altogether. Their footsteps pounded out a rhythm as they sprinted across the hard-packed dirt. The trees were far apart. Abigail chose a path that led them downward. Though he trusted that she knew where she was going, their path seemed a bit random.

As they ran, and the sound of the dogs faded, the hermit's story played at the corners of his mind. The man must have been deeply in love with his wife, had seen it as his job to protect her. He didn't know the circumstances of the car accident, but the man clearly blamed himself for it, and it had driven him into solitude. Though he lived and worked with people all around him, Jesse had chosen a solitary life, too.

Abigail stumbled. Jesse reached out to catch her before she fell.

She grabbed his arm and locked him in her gaze as she caught her breath. "Thank you."

He thought again of the hermit. What did it do to a man whose choices led to the death of a woman he loved? It was a heavy burden to love someone and lose them. The guilt that he could have done something more to save Melissa plagued him always.

His heart pounded against his rib cage as he sucked in air. He squeezed her elbow. "Let's go."

The dogs grew closer, relentless in their pursuit of their targets.

SIX

Abigail was grateful for the full belly and renewed energy. Though she avoided the trail because it would be too easy to track them, she guided them down the mountain. They walked and jogged throughout the morning into the late afternoon. When they'd gone for at least an hour without hearing the dogs, she stopped to rest at the edge of an open area, finding a log to sit down on.

Jesse sat beside her. "Where are we exactly?"

She tilted her head toward the sky. They still had four or five hours of daylight. "If we keep going straight through the night, we're probably about twelve hours from the trailhead."

He pulled the water bottle from the backpack and offered her a drink. "Then that's what we should do."

She took several gulps of water and then handed him the bottle. "I can take us sort of parallel to the trail. It's a little more treacherous but we'll be less likely to be spotted."

"That guy back there, living by himself. You knew who he was." He drank from the water bottle.

"The accident happened when I was little, but it was

big news around the Northwest. There were all kinds of rumors and stories. That he had been drinking. That the driver they collided with had been drinking. Who knows what the truth was."

"He must have loved his wife, felt responsible." Jesse closed the spout on the water bottle and put it back in the pack.

His voice was tinged with emotion that she hadn't heard before. "Something about him got to you, huh?"

"Sad, really. Living up there all alone," he said.

"That man died a long time ago. He just forgot to stop breathing." She studied him for a moment.

Jesse's features intensified, and the shadows on his cheekbones becoming more defined. He cleared his throat as though he were thinking deeply about something. "I never thought of it that way."

She wondered what was going through his mind. Why the encounter with the isolated stranger had caused such a shift for him.

Her early suspicions of him had been tainted by her own betrayal by Brent. And she'd been on her guard about wanting to show him she could do her job as well as any man.

One side of his mouth curved up in a smile. "What are you thinking?"

She shook her head, feeling a connection to him and a sudden vulnerability. She shut down the emotion as quickly as it had invaded her awareness. She jumped to her feet. "I was thinking we should get moving." Yes, he was a human being who probably had his own struggles and a story to tell, but she still didn't know what to think about him. Had he kept her alive because he needed her expertise to get out of these mountains? Or was he who he said he was, a DEA agent who'd been framed? The jury was still out. For now, they needed to focus on getting back to Fort Madison and to her predictable life, though she wasn't sure what that life would look like without Brent and the plans they'd made together.

Jesse rose to his feet, as well.

She stepped away from the trees. From this vantage point, she could see the river snaking through the mountains. Though not visible from here, Fort Madison was just beyond the far mountain range. They had a long trek ahead of them.

They ran at a steady pace without stopping until the sky turned charcoal and then black. Darkness slowed their pace.

They walked side by side and chose their path more carefully, winding around trees and bushes and across rockier, more open terrain. From time to time, they heard the dogs baying. The barking made her heart beat a little more intensely. Because the sound echoed off the mountains, it was hard to discern where the dogs were exactly.

She got caught up in the rhythm of their footsteps and took advantage of the chance to find out more about Jesse. "You never answered my question. Did you always want to be a DEA agent?"

They walked for several more feet before he said anything. He ducked to avoid a low-hanging tree branch. An owl hooted somewhere in the distance. "I just sort of drifted into it and found out I was good at it. Did a tour in Afghanistan, was a cop for a while. I really can't talk about my work, Abigail."

So he wasn't about to give her any details about his life. "What can you talk about?"

"I thought I was supposed to be the extrovert?" His voice held just a note of teasing.

"Guess the silence was starting to bother me, too."

They walked on for hours as the sky grew even darker. The steep mountains turned to more rolling hills. When she looked all around her, there were no flashlights shining in the distance. That didn't mean they could let their guard down, though.

She stopped short and pointed off in the distance at the twinkling lights of Fort Madison so far away it would be easy to miss them unless you knew to look for them. "Not much of a city."

"But it's a welcome sight," Jesse said. "Now all we have to do is walk toward the lights, right?"

His comment sent a little wave of fear through her. What would he do if he didn't need her expertise anymore? "We still have a long way to hike. We'll go down into a valley in a little bit. Then you won't be able to see the lights anymore."

"I'm glad I'm with someone who knows the way," said Jesse.

They stopped to rest and eat handfuls of candy. Jesse remained vigilant, pacing in an arc to look all around them. "I don't see any signs of the thugs. That kind of worries me. What are they up to?"

Her chest squeezed tight at the question. She jumped to her feet. "The best thing for us to do is to keep moving."

As they drew closer to civilization, the unspoken suspicion about Jesse sat like a rock in her stomach.

When they wandered down into the valley, the sound of a helicopter reached her ears. She could see the tiny flashing light far in the distance. The chopper didn't come anywhere near them. The lights disappeared behind the mountain they had just come down.

"That could be anybody, right?" Jesse's voice held a note of tension as they stood together in the darkness.

She trudged ahead. "Yeah, people hire choppers all the time." Tension knotted through her chest. "Night flights are a little unusual, though."

"There wasn't one available for hire when I looked into it. You never would have been dragged into this if I'd been able to go that route."

Though she could not see his expression in the dark, his tone sounded genuinely apologetic. "Hopefully, all of this will just be a memory for me soon."

Jesse walked a little faster as they rose up out of the valley and the lights of Fort Madison became visible again. Their path intersected with the trail.

"This looks familiar," said Jesse.

"Yes, the trail leads right into town." Which meant he didn't need her anymore. She tensed, waiting for his response.

"Probably be smarter not to be out in the open, right?"

She pointed. "We can zigzag through the trees that run parallel to the trail."

"Let's go, then." He patted her shoulder. "I can't thank you enough for all your help."

If he was who he said he was, a lawman who had been wronged, she would be back at home within hours. She stared at him for a long moment, unable to discern his features in the predawn light. "Let's get moving."

She darted toward the trees and trotted along the soft ground, slowed only by the lack of light.

As the sun came up, the forest thinned. She could see

the outskirts of Fort Madison, some scattered cabins and barns still far away but discernable. Though the town was visible now, they still had hours of hiking ahead of them. She ran even faster. A weight seemed to lift off her as they drew closer to town. "My place is closer than the Big Sky Outfitters office. My car is there. I jog into the office most days. You can make calls from there, or I can take you where you need to go."

He stopped for a second. His forehead creased. "Yes, I guess I need to figure out my next move." He patted his pocket, where he'd put the hard drive.

They hiked for several more hours as the sun moved across the sky.

Her home, which was a thirty-foot camper trailer, was on a piece of land just outside town. She nearly cried when they came up over a hill and its silvery exterior glistened in the noon light.

"That's where you live?"

"Yes, I'm really into the tiny-house concept and traveling light. The outdoors are my living room," she said. Also, she had thought she and Brent would be buying a house together once they were married.

She felt a heaviness as they got closer to her home. What kind of life was she coming back to here, anyway? If she stayed and worked in Fort Madison, she'd run into Brent sooner or later.

They jogged the remaining distance. She got her key from underneath the trailer, where the trim was curved enough to hold an object, and unlocked the door. "I just need to get my car keys. You can come inside. I can make us some food."

She opened her trailer. Outdoor gear, backpacks,

tents, sleeping bags and cross-country skis were scattered throughout the tiny space.

Jesse stepped inside. "Looks like you're prepared for almost anything."

The comment felt like a barb, though she knew he hadn't intended it that way. Because she'd grown up with older brothers, she had learned to compete with them on equal footing. The memory of Brent's parting words to her echoed in her head.

Honestly, Abigail, you're almost too capable of doing everything for yourself. Why do you even need me?

Brent's words still hurt.

"Have a seat." While Jesse settled in, she opened the refrigerator. She pulled some chili out of the freezer and popped it in the microwave, letting it heat through while she sliced some cheese, then got crackers from the cupboard. She brought the cheese and crackers to the table and said, "I make my chili kind of spicy. I hope that's okay."

He offered her a warm smile. "I love spicy."

His smile made her heart skip a beat. There hadn't been much reason to smile up until now. Once the chili was heated through, she dished it up and placed a steaming bowl in front of Jesse beside the plate of sliced cheese and crackers. She sat down opposite him and picked up her spoon. "So, what are you going to do now?"

Jesse's features hardened. "I need to look at the contents of the hard drive first." He let out a heavy breath. "Then I have to find someone I can trust with the information, someone who will believe me."

He seemed distressed.

"And that won't be easy to do, huh?"

He brought the spoon up to his mouth. "Good chili."

He still wasn't going to talk about his work. What did it matter to her? In another hour, he would be on his way to parts unknown. She watched him eat the chili.

"Delicious," he said. "You're a good cook."

"Not really. But I have a couple of specialties I do really well."

He scraped the bottom of the bowl with his spoon. "Well, I could live on chili like this. Not too wimpy, just the right amount of kick to it."

His compliment made her feel like she was glowing from the inside. It was nice to have her cooking appreciated. "Would you like another bowl?"

"Sure. Fill 'er up." He pushed the bowl across the table and licked his lips.

She set a steaming bowl in front of him and then sat down to finish the rest of her first serving.

He raised his spoon. "To good food and good company." His voice took on a warm tone as he looked her right in the eyes. "And to a job well done, Abigail."

When he looked at her that way, her heart fluttered a little. "I know you are who you say you are. I'm sorry I didn't believe you at first." If he had wanted to do her harm, he would have by now.

He put his spoon on the table. "I understand why you thought what you did. I'm sure I looked like just another one of the bad guys."

She realized then that saying goodbye would be harder than she'd thought it would be. A bond had formed between them. You don't spend a few days running for your life with someone and not feel a connection to them. "I hope everything turns out okay for you."

They finished eating and she grabbed her car keys off the hook by the door. Jesse stepped outside first. She shuffled around the camper, looking for her purse.

She swung open the door to a view of Jesse standing with his hands in the air. Her heart pounded faster as she shifted in the doorway to see two of the thugs from the mountain, Pretty Boy and Eddy, holding their guns on Jesse. The chopper must have gone up there to get them.

Pretty Boy turned his gun on Abigail. "Get out here and stand by your partner. We're missing some product. What did you do with it?"

He must be talking about the drugs the hermit had taken. She wasn't about to put that lonely old man in danger.

"We didn't take your drugs," said Jesse.

"We'll see about that." Pretty Boy tilted his head toward Eddy, who yanked Abigail out of the trailer and then stepped inside.

She could hear Eddy moving around in her trailer, searching.

She hurried to stand beside Jesse. Of course, they'd figured out where she lived.

Eddy poked his head out. "Nothing in here."

Pretty Boy stalked toward them. "You must have hidden it somewhere on the mountain. We can make you talk." Before she could even fully absorb what was happening, he lifted his gun and landed a blow to the side of her head.

Jesse came to, thinking that he was on a boat in bad weather. He opened his eyes. As he was regaining consciousness, the jittery swaying motion of the van they were in made him think they were at sea in a storm. Now he saw his surroundings for what they really were. He and Abigail had been knocked unconscious and tossed into the back of some kind of service van. There was a back door and no windows. Both sides of the van had shelving that at one time must have contained tools of some kind. Now they looked mostly bare.

A toolbox vibrated across the floor as the van bumped down the road. A water bottle rolled toward him. He picked it up, unscrewed the top and smelled the clear liquid inside. No odor. He took a tentative sip. Water. The men who had kidnapped them had wanted to keep them alive—for now, anyway.

Beside him, Abigail was still unconscious.

He groaned. The last thing he'd wanted was for her to be mixed up in this all over again.

Abigail stirred. "My head hurts."

He patted her shoulder. "Sit up slowly."

She blinked, touched her head and then sat up. "What happened?"

"It appears that we are going for a bit of a road trip. I have no idea where we are." He could only guess at how long they'd been unconscious. Several hours at least.

His last memory was of lunging at the man who had knocked out Abigail, and then his own world had gone dark.

"They didn't kill us outright because they want to find out where those drugs are, right?"

He had to hand it to Abigail. She was sharp at figuring things out. He suspected the road trip was about taking them to someone whose methods were more *persuasive* in getting information out of people. But he kept that theory to himself.

"If those other guys find the old man, they'll know we don't have the drugs."

Though the old man seemed pretty savvy at surviving, he hoped the thugs didn't hurt him and would just trade the drugs for whatever the hermit wanted.

Abigail pulled her knees up to her chest.

"I'm really sorry. You did your job. This should have been over for you back at your trailer," he said.

Abigail met his apology with silence.

He didn't blame her for being upset.

The van rolled to a stop. He heard voices and other cars. He inched toward the back doors and rattled the handle. Locked, of course.

Abigail tilted her head. "We must be at a gas station or something."

Jesse slid open the drawers of the toolbox, desperately looking for something that might pry open the door. He found a rusty wrench.

Abigail had jumped to her feet and was running her hands along the shelving.

The door of the van swung open; a bag was tossed in.

Jesse leaped across the expanse of the van toward the door just as he heard the lock click back into place. Both of them stared at the bag, which had nothing written on it. A grease mark had formed at the bottom.

"It looks like dinner or…breakfast? I'm not sure how long we've been in here, but my stomach is growling, so it's got to be at least five or six hours since we had that chili."

Jesse shrugged. "The bag is probably not going to explode, right?"

"Right." Abigail sat back down on the floor and reached for the bag. She pulled out an item wrapped in paper and opened it up to reveal a burger. She handed it to Jesse and then lifted the second one out for herself. The final container was filled with french fries.

Jesse grabbed the water bottle and held up a french fry. "Here's to good food and great service."

Grease dripped from the bottom of the bun as Abigail took a big bite. "Yes, we'll have to make sure to leave a big tip."

He appreciated that she was so willing to play along in what was truly a dismal situation.

He offered her a drink from the water bottle. She took several gulps.

The meal was greasy but satisfying. He leaned against the far wall of the van as it rolled down the road, swaying from side to side when it gained speed, probably to pass other cars.

Abigail finished her last bite of burger.

"I left you some fries," he said.

She picked up the carton and scooted over to sit by him. She shoved the fries toward him. "I can't eat all these."

He took a fry and chewed. As they grew colder, the fries became less appetizing. Abigail set them to one side, drew her knees up to her chest and tilted her head. Minutes ticked by with neither of them saying anything.

Outside, he detected the hum of other cars whizzing by. The van slowed down at one point, maybe due to traffic or because they were going through a town. He had no way of knowing for sure.

"You think our hosts would have at least thrown in a deck of cards," he said, trying to keep his tone light. Might as well have a conversation. Silence allowed too much opportunity for worry and speculation. He had to keep his head in this situation.

She leaned a little closer to him. "Jesse, what are we going to do?"

The fear in her voice touched something deep inside him. He longed to make her feel safe, but he couldn't lie.

He picked up the wrench he'd found. "We're going to look for an opportunity to escape. They have to stop sooner or later, and they probably have plans to pull us out of here."

"And do what with us?"

"Let's not go there," he said.

"They think we stashed those drugs somewhere. I'm sure not going to put that old man in danger." Her voice had become more frantic.

He gave her hand a quick squeeze. "We need to focus on waiting for the right moment and being ready when it comes. Did you find anything we could use on those shelves?"

"Just some old rags." She sounded distraught.

Guilt washed through him. This was not her fight. "We'll figure this out." And yet, she hadn't turned on him or blamed him.

Again, the silence fell around them. After maybe an hour, she lay down on her side and rested facing him. He pulled off his jacket, took out the hard drive, put it in his zippered pants pocket and folded the jacket. "You can use my coat for a pillow."

"Thank you." She lifted her head and he slid it underneath her.

He remained awake and vigilant. For the most part, the van moved at a consistent pace. They must have been on a road or highway without much other traffic.

Abigail stirred in her sleep. He'd gotten used to seeing her with her hat pulled down over part of her face.
In an understated way, she was an attractive woman.
Though she wore no makeup, she had a sort of natural
beauty and inner glow.

Her eyes fluttered open. "You're staring at me."

"Sorry. There were no good shows on the televi-
sion," he said.

She laughed. "Yeah, it's kind of a sensory-deprivation
tank in here." She sat up.

"I was just thinking I'm so sorry for ripping you out
of your life in Fort Madison. You probably have family
and maybe a boyfriend."

"My family is in Idaho." She frowned. "Had a boyfriend, past tense. A fiancé actually." Her voice was
filled with anguish. She tilted her head. Sadness saturated her words. "I don't want to talk about it."

He wasn't sure why he'd even broached the subject.
He supposed he was curious about who she was beyond
what he'd seen of her working as a guide.

"What about you? Do you have family? A girlfriend?"

"I have an aloe vera plant named George. That's
about it. George doesn't mind that I'm gone for long
periods of time."

"No family?"

"A sister I talk to on holidays. I usually go see her
and her kids once a year."

"Mom and Dad?"

He wasn't used to talking about himself this much.
The question struck a nerve. "Dad was a pilot. I guess
that's where I first got the flying bug. He and Mom got
caught in a storm. It was a small plane."

"I'm sorry." A quiet hush fell around them. It wasn't an uncomfortable silence. It felt more like a respectful response for what he had just told her. "How old were you when that happened?"

"Just turned eighteen. Long time ago." And after that, Melissa. The pain was just right beneath the surface. He hadn't really talked to anyone about this. It surprised him how easy it was to open up to her. He wondered, too, if he was a lot like the hermit—dead but still breathing.

The van slowed. The tires made a different sound. They were no longer on pavement. Gravel crunched beneath the tires and the van came to a stop.

Jesse took in a breath and wrapped his fingers around the wrench. He moved so he was crouching by the van doors. This was it. Something was about to happen.

SEVEN

Abigail's heart beat faster as she hurried across the van floor and settled on the opposite side of the doors. When the doors opened, they'd be ready.

She could hear music playing in the cab of the van, something jazzy and turned down to a low volume. Once in a while a voice rose up with one- or two-word sentences. Then the music shut off. Were the men waiting for something or someone?

At least five minutes passed. Abigail repositioned herself before her legs cramped.

More tires crunched underneath the gravel. Another car must have pulled into where the van was parked. A different kind of music was playing from the other car, something with a driving, pounding beat, music that was meant to intimidate. The van shook from the intensity of the doors being slammed shut.

The music continued to play. Voices rose above it. Some sort of argument was taking place. Men shouted swear words.

The music stopped.

Abigail heard a sort of zinging sound. And then the rat-a-tat of guns being fired. More shouting. Footsteps crunched on gravel and moved closer to them.

She pressed her hand against the van door as her heart raced and every muscle tensed. More gunfire. Bullets tore through the van, letting in round slivers of light.

"Get down." Jesse reached out and tugged on the top part of her shoulder. She was flat on her stomach with her hands on her head as the gunfire continued. Paralyzed by fear, she remained motionless.

As abruptly as it had started, the shooting ceased. Still lying flat, she lifted her head a few inches. She could see holes in the van walls where the bullets had gone through—four of them.

Footsteps crunched on gravel, growing closer. "Check the back. See if the merchandise is there." The volume of man's voice indicated he was outside the van. The voice was not Pretty Boy's or Eddy's.

"Now's our chance," said Jesse. He raised the wrench.

Trying to shake off the shock of having been caught in the middle of a gun battle, Abigail resumed her position on the opposite side of the doors. She gained courage from the look of determination on Jesse's face as he raised the wrench.

Some sort of latch or lever on the van was being twisted around, and then one of the doors swung open. Jesse leaped on top of the man who had opened the door. She jumped out of the van after him. The two men rolled around on the ground. Jesse had dropped the wrench in the struggle and she scrambled toward it. Her hands wrapped around the cold metal of the handle just as someone came up behind her. She whirled around, swinging the wrench. A tall man she had never seen before stepped out of range and pulled out a gun, which he aimed at her.

Abigail heard the resounding slap of flesh against flesh as Jesse and the other man exchanged blows and rolled around on the ground.

The tall man shouted something in Spanish at the other man, which made him stop fighting with Jesse. A bit ruffled from the fight, the short man stepped away from Jesse. The tall man pointed his gun at Abigail and Jesse, indicating they needed to stand to one side. The short man peered inside the van and shook his head.

The two men exchanged words in Spanish and shook their heads. The tall one got behind the wheel of the car they had come in. The short man said something to Jesse in Spanish and then shot the tires out on the van before running over to the car and getting in.

Both of them stood watching as the car pulled out on the road, growing smaller and smaller in the waning early-evening light.

Abigail let out a heavy breath. Her heart was still pounding from all the excitement. "What was that about?"

"Those guys thought they were intercepting a drug shipment. They must have been rival dealers who got bad info that these guys were hauling drugs."

"What did that man say to you?"

"He said he didn't want to complicate his life by killing us, and dealing in human cargo was not his thing," said Jesse.

She pointed at the deflated tires. "But he didn't want us following them, either."

"You stay here. I want to see what the condition of the two men who were driving the van is." He hurried around to the front end of the van, out of her view, returning several minutes later. He shook his head. "Both are dead. The guns have been taken off of them."

Abigail stared up and down the long, lonely stretch of road as her breath caught in her throat. So Pretty Boy and Eddy were dead. She knew they were not good men, but they probably had people in their lives who loved them all the same. Someone would hurt over them being gone.

"Where are we?" It was only a two-lane rural road. As far as the eye could see, it was all rolling hills—no fences, no houses, not even a cow or a barn.

"What does it look like to you?"

She shrugged. "Kind of like the badlands of eastern Montana, but I don't have a lot to go off of. We could be in Wyoming or even farther south. All of the western US has parts that are really remote. All I know is that we are not in downtown Los Angeles or Seattle."

Jesse nodded. "It was morning when they grabbed us at your trailer." He tilted his head. "Must only have a few hours of daylight left now."

She nodded. None of that information made it any clearer as to where they were. When she studied the road in either direction, she couldn't even see a sign that indicated what the next town or city was.

"Wait here." Jesse moved around to the cab of the van and opened up the doors, probably looking for anything they might be able to use. He tossed a coat in her direction. "I imagine it will get colder as the night wears on."

She grabbed the coat. "So we walk?" She knew the minute she spoke that it was a dumb question. They sure weren't going to fly out of here.

Jesse retrieved his jacket from the back of the van and joined her by the edge of the road. "Sooner or later, we'll run into something, or someone will come along." He touched her back lightly and pointed. "Those men headed north on this road. That means they were headed toward some place. That's our best bet for running into civilization."

She tried not to look at the two dead bodies as she and Jesse made their way toward the road. "Those guys were taking us somewhere. What happens when they don't show up with us?"

Jesse let out a heavy breath. "I imagine whoever was expecting us will come looking for us."

That reality sent a wave of fear through her. When would this all end? As the sun descended lower in the sky, she focused on the tapping of their footfalls, trying not to let her imagination get the best of her.

It would be a while before whomever they were being delivered to came out looking for them and found the two dead men. This road would be the first place they'd come searching.

Jesse shoved his hands in his pockets and walked beside her.

"So, do you suppose your aloe vera plant is missing you about now?"

Jesse laughed.

"I should have been back by now from guiding you in. My boss and his wife are out of town, but some of my friends will start to wonder when I don't show up for church stuff…and choir practice." Although people probably wouldn't expect her to show up at choir practice with Brent's new girlfriend there. Really, she didn't even like the idea of going back to Fort Madison and having to face all that pain.

"No," he said, a note of sadness coming into his voice. "No one is wondering where I am."

"Someone might figure out I'm missing." She choked on her words. "But they won't even know where to look. They'll be searching the mountains and trails by Fort Madison."

Jesse wrapped his arm around her back and gave her shoulder a quick squeeze before letting go. "We're going to figure this out."

"I feel like we should pray," she said, not sure how he would react. She felt like she was at the end of her rope. Prayer seemed like the only thing that would help them now.

"Sure, you can pray."

"You don't pray anymore?"

"No, I do. I did." He stared off into the distance. "I still pray when I get myself into a tight spot. It's just that I was married years ago and she—she died. After that and losing my parents, my faith kind of went dormant, I guess."

She was honored that he had shared something so deeply private with her. Faith could be a fragile thing. Her loss was nothing compared to what he must have been through. "I understand how prayer could be hard after all that."

They walked, not saying much at all for at least an hour, still not seeing any sign of civilization.

Stars twinkled as the sky turned from gray to black. The wind blew, creating a rushing sound over the grassy fields that bordered the road. She zipped up the extra coat Jesse had given her. It was a fleece-lined jean jacket that had an odd fruity odor, but she was grateful for the extra warmth as the temperature dropped.

"I see a light over there." Jesse tugged at her elbow and pointed.

A single light bobbed across the distant hills. It was too dark and too far away to discern anything else. "That might be one person camping or out looking for a lost dog. They could be gone by the time we get over there."

"And there might be a cabin there or something. If we stay on the road, we risk an encounter with the men who are going to come looking for the dead guys," Jesse said. "And so far, we have yet to encounter another human being or even a sign of another human."

Clearly, they were on some back road that was not used much. Abigail fought off the despair that threatened to overtake her. She'd been lost before. She'd been uncertain of which way to go before.

She breathed in a quick, silent prayer. "Okay."

Under the cover of darkness, they veered off the road and hiked toward where they'd seen the light. They walked up and down the rolling hills, across a dry creek bed and through a fledgling patch of evergreens. The only signs that humans had ever been in this part of the world were a rusty soda can and a plastic bag that could have blown from somewhere else.

The land here was much flatter, with only sparse vegetation, unlike the high mountains outside Fort Madison.

They came to a hill that looked down into a valley. Though the moon provided some light, everything was mostly covered in shadows. As they hiked into the valley and back up the other side, the tinkling sound of a creek was a welcome break from the monotony of the landscape.

They stopped at the creek and took a drink by cupping their hands and filling them with cool water. They had forgotten to take the water bottle out of the back of the van. The burger and fries they'd been given by their captors had worn off long ago.

Abigail stood up. She thought she heard the barking of a dog far in the distance, but it might have been just wishful thinking.

A much more distinctive sound came from behind her—the back-and-forth ratcheting of a shotgun as the cartridge slid into the chamber.

A male voice filled with fear and anger pelted her back. "The two of you better just hold it right there. Put your hands up where I can see them."

Jesse's leg muscles tensed—he was ready for fight or flight, whatever the occasion called for now that a shotgun was pointed at his back. Not again. Hadn't they just been through this with the hermit?

Jesse let out a heavy exhale to clear his mind. The first option was always to negotiate yourself out of the violent threat. "We're not here to hurt you. We're lost. If you would just let me turn around and speak to you." He needed to know what he was dealing with.

"Stay right where you are, both of you." The man sounded more afraid than bent on violence.

The distant bleating of sheep and the sound of a dog barking reached him. Was this man a sheepherder?

"We're not armed. We don't want to rob you or anything. We're lost—we're trying to find our way back to…" He had no idea what state they were even in. If they explained why, of course it would sound nefarious and far-fetched.

"Nobody comes out this far," said the man. "Unless they're up to something."

Abigail cleared her throat. "Please, at least let us put our hands down."

After a long pause, the man replied, "All right, and turn around slowly."

Both of them dropped their arms and turned to face the man, who held a shotgun on them. Though his face was covered in shadow and he sported a hefty beard, Jesse guessed the man was in his late twenties or early thirties.

"You're a sheepherder? Out here by yourself for long periods of time?" Abigail's were words filled with compassion. She must have understood something about why the man was so paranoid.

"I'm not alone." The man whistled. A moment later, a border collie came bounding over the hill and sat at attention at the man's feet. "Cosette keeps me company."

Great. Another hermit.

"We need to get to the nearest town," said Jesse. "Where would that be?"

The man cocked his head to one side. "You don't know? Did your car break down or what? Your story has all kinds of holes in it. I can't take you into town. I can't leave the sheep."

Jesse could feel himself losing patience. "If you could just point us in the right direction. Tell us where we are?"

The border collie emitted a low growl, apparently not happy about the rising tension.

The sheepherder adjusted the shotgun, so the barrel pointed right at Jesse's chest. "Are you on drugs or something? What have you been doing that you don't even know where you are?"

Jesse clenched his teeth. "Look, buddy, no one gives good answers with a gun pointed at them."

"I know our story sounds a little crazy," Abigail said softly.

The man lowered the gun an inch or so. "More than a little crazy."

"I understand that you can't leave the sheep." She glanced down at the dog. "Cosette. That's a pretty name."

The man's squared shoulders relaxed a little. "Cozy for short."

"After the character in *Les Misérables*?"

"Yeah." The man let the gun fall to his side.

"One of my favorites, too," said Abigail. "What is your name?"

"Edward."

"Edward. I'm Abigail, and this is my friend Jesse."

Abigail had forged a connection with the man and calmed him down. He had to commend Abigail on her negotiation skills, which had never been his strong suit. He was a man of action, not words. Just like with the hermit, having her around had come in handy.

The man addressed Abigail. "Sorry for the full-on assault. I haven't heard another human voice in months. It just seems like the only reason for someone to come out here is because they're up to no good. Guess I'm wound a little tight."

Jesse wondered what Edward was referencing, about people being up to no good.

"I assure you, we just need to be pointed in the right direction," Abigail said.

Edward stepped a little closer toward Abigail. "Like I said, I haven't had any company since my employee dropped off supplies. You must be hungry. Why don't you come back to the camp?"

Jesse was starting to feel like he was invisible.

"That sounds like a plan, Edward," said Abigail.

Edward whistled and Cozy took off running, disappearing over the hill from where she'd come. "Follow the border collie. Camp is just up this way."

Edward had a knowledge of literature, and he seemed well-spoken. Jesse wondered what had led him to such a solitary life.

They hiked over the hill. In the valley below, a flock of sheep grazed while Cozy kept watch on the rim of the hill.

The sheep wagon was a camper that looked like it had been built in the fifties and restored. Edward had a cookstove set up on a table. He disappeared inside the camper.

"I wonder if I'm even going to get fed." Jesse gave Abigail a friendly punch on the shoulder.

"What do you mean?"

"He's only got eyes for you."

"I imagine this is a very lonely life out here." Abigail crossed her arms over her chest. "Obviously, nothing can come of it. We're just passing through."

Edward returned, holding several cans of food. He offered Abigail a big smile. "Sorry, don't have much in the way of fresh food."

Seeing Edward smile like that at Abigail caused a twinge of an unfamiliar emotion to rise up in Jesse. What was that feeling? Jealousy?

He glanced over at Abigail. Her hair had come loose

from the braid and was framing her face in soft waves. She was pretty, but what he liked was the complexity of who she was as a person. His first impression of her had been that she was all hard edges, but now she seemed softer, capable of a deep compassion. Maybe it was just because of what they had been through together, but he felt himself drawn to her.

Edward opened the cans, lit the cookstove and dumped the contents of the cans into the pan that rested on the burner. After the meal had heated for a while, he left again and returned with plates and utensils.

"I only have two plates," said Edward.

Jesse leaned close to Abigail and said under his breath, "See, I told you I wasn't going to get fed."

Abigail elbowed him in the stomach and gave him a raised-eyebrow reprimand. "Jesse and I can share a plate."

Edward offered Abigail his only chair while the two men sat on the ground and ate the beans that had been mixed with tomatoes.

Jesse took a couple of bites and then handed the plate to Abigail. "What did you mean when you said that most people you encounter are out here for nefarious purposes?"

"We're about ninety miles from the Bakken oil fields in North Dakota. Lot of drugs and people being trafficked through there."

Though he'd never worked in the area, Jesse was familiar with the extent of the drug problem in the Bakken. A high concentration of men working long hard hours, not many families or women and confined living quarters made it a ripe area for all sorts of criminal activity. Eddy and Pretty Boy must have been taking Abigail and Jesse there.

"I can see why you were so suspicious of us." Abigail handed the plate back to Jesse.

"The company is nice." Again with the smiles at Abigail. "I'm used to being around people. I grew up on the East Coast. Flunked out of college, made a lot of bad choices. Thought if I came out here, I could get my head cleared up, figure out my life, maybe do some writing."

Edward sure was volunteering a lot of personal information. "And how has that worked out for you?"

Edward seemed almost shocked at Jesse's question, like he'd forgotten he was present. Jesse himself was surprised that his voice had a little bit of an edge to it.

"That was three years ago. I guess I still haven't figured my life out."

They finished their meal and Jesse burst to his feet. "We should get moving." He handed Edward the empty plate. "I don't suppose you have any way to communicate with the outside world."

Edward shook his head. "No cell towers out here. I like the quiet."

"If you'll point us in the right direction, we need to get to the nearest town." Jesse wasn't sure what they would do after that.

"The main highway is to the northeast, about three miles." Edward pointed. "You should hit a small town called Stubenville."

Jesse's mind lit up. Now he knew where they were. A retired agent named Dale lived about an hour outside Stubenville. Dale might be able to help him figure out how to make the case for his innocence, see for sure what was on the hard drive and find a way to send Abigail home safely.

"Wait just a minute. I have something for you." Edward disappeared inside the camper and returned a moment later, holding two granola bars. "It might be a while before someone picks you up and…" He held up a flashlight. "You might need this." He handed the bars and flashlight to Abigail.

"Thanks, Edward. I hope everything turns out okay for you," she said.

They turned and headed up the hill. She handed Jesse the flashlight, which he clicked on. It illuminated a swath of land in front of them. After they had walked for several minutes in silence, she spoke up. "You were a little rude back there. Why?"

"I don't know. Edward was fawning over you a little too much."

But he did know why. He was starting to have feelings for Abigail. He hadn't realized it until another man had shown interest in her. They were not feelings he could ever act on. They were from different worlds. As soon as they got back to civilization, he needed to put Abigail back on a bus to Fort Madison.

All the same, he had to at least admit to himself that he admired, even liked her.

EIGHT

Though she couldn't put her finger on it, Abigail sensed that something had shifted between her and Jesse. "Edward wasn't my type."

"What is your type?"

Brent had been her boyfriend for three years, and she had known him since grade school. They'd been engaged for over a year. There had been boys in high school who had been more friends than anything, nothing serious. "I guess I don't know anymore. Don't know if I ever knew."

"What do you mean?"

Talking about Brent was painful. She'd only shared her heartache with her mom and God. But Jesse had shared something much more traumatic about his life. "Guess I'm just kind of naive. I moved to Fort Madison because my fiancé got a job there. I thought we'd get married and raise our kids there. I never questioned that until a while ago, the guy I was engaged to decided he wanted to be with someone else."

"That's tough. Really, Abigail, I'm sorry for all that pain," he said.

"Yeah, I got this idea in my head that my life was going to turn out a certain way," she said.

"Everyone thinks that. That life has a certain trajectory. High school, college, marriage, kids, retirement. No one factors in the loss and the derailment."

Jesse's profound words sank in deep as they walked on through the darkness, until they could hear the sound of an occasional car going by on the road up ahead.

"Will it be safe to be close to the main road? Won't they be looking for us?"

"Probably, but it's nighttime. It's a stretch of road to cover and there's no way we'll catch a ride into Stubenville if we aren't on that road."

Jesse's reasoning was sound. All the same, fear formed a knot at the base of her neck as they got closer to the road. Once they reached pavement, they walked on the shoulder.

"We'll be all right," he said.

He must have picked up on her anxiety, which surprised her. She thought she was pretty good at hiding it. Was he starting to be tuned in to her feelings and moods? The notion scared her a little. If he cared about her feelings, he probably cared about her in a deeper way than just feeling responsible for her safety.

"This is a rural community, probably lots of farms around here. Most farm people will stop if they see us walking," she said. "I just don't know how many people are going to be out at night." She talked to get her racing thoughts off the hamster wheel in her head. So what if Jesse was tuned in to her feelings? Nothing was going to come of it.

"That's good. All we need is one car to come along headed toward Stubenville."

Their shoulders bumped now and then as they walked side by side. Their footsteps made a sort of squishy, crunching sound on the loose gravel at the edge of the road.

They passed a field where cows grazed and rested. There were no lights anywhere on the landscape. No sign of a farmhouse. She crossed her arms over her chest as the night grew colder.

Then she heard the car in the distance. When she looked over her shoulder, the golden headlights were two tiny dots that disappeared as the car descended the hill.

"What if it's one of those men looking for us?"

"It's a chance we gotta take. Or we have a long walk ahead of us in the dark." He leaned a little closer to her. "We'll both keep our radar up. Talk to the guy for a few minutes before we get in the car. If either of us gets a bad feeling, we'll step away and bolt."

The car grew louder, and the headlights became visible again.

The plan was fraught with danger. "Should we have some sort of signal?"

"Just squeeze my elbow," he said. "And I'll do the same for you if I sense any red flags."

As the car drew even closer, Abigail's heart pounded a little faster.

Holding the flashlight, Jesse waved his arms in the air.

The car whizzed past.

Abigail experienced a dark moment when it looked like the car wasn't even going to stop. The driver hit the brakes with such intensity, the car slid sideways.

They both looked at each other and then ran up to the car. Jesse stood by the driver's-side window and Abigail positioned herself behind him. She peered over her shoulder at the side of the road. If the driver was armed, they could bolt for the ditch and then head into the shelter of the cluster of trees.

The driver's window came down. Though her face was covered in shadow, the driver looked to be a middle-aged woman.

"Did you folks break down?"

"Yes, something like that," Jesse said.

From inside the car, she heard the sound of two girls arguing. Abigail breathed a sigh of relief. Chances were this mom was not someone connected to the drug trade.

"Quiet, girls." Once the fighting between the two kids stopped, the woman gripped the steering wheel and stared through the windshield. "Huh, I didn't see any broken-down cars back there." Suspicion clouded the woman's words.

"Please, if we could just get a ride into town," he said.

Abigail stepped a little closer to the car so the woman could see her. "It's dark. It would be easy to miss seeing the car."

"That's true," said the woman. She glanced at Jesse and then at Abigail. She shrugged. "You'll have to ride in the back with one of my crabby daughters. It's been a long day for us."

"Thank you. We appreciate it." Abigail put her hand forward so the woman could shake it. "I'm Abigail and this is Jesse."

"Pleased to meet you," said the woman.

Once they were in the car, the woman pulled out onto the road. "My name is Sandra. But everyone calls me Sis. These are my daughters, Arielle and Dawn."

The older daughter sat in the front seat. She looked

to be in her teens. Arielle gave the two passengers a nod and then put earbuds in her ears and faced forward. Jesse and Abigail sat on either side of Dawn, who held a doll in her lap. The younger daughter was maybe seven or eight years old.

Sis glanced at them in the rearview mirror, probably still wondering if she had made the right choice. "Like I said, it's been a long day for us. My girls competed in a gymnastics tournament up in Dickenson."

Dawn lifted her doll in the air and then hugged it tight. "We didn't win."

"Arielle got fourth place on the balance beam," said Sis.

Abigail stared out at the area bordering the road. They whizzed past a historical marker. She saw lights in the distance that must be farms.

Dawn chatted away about the tournament, her lunch, the boy who was mean to her at school and anything else that popped into her head, and then she broke into song.

When there was a lull in Dawn's monologue, Sis piped up. "Dawn will talk your ear off if you let her. Arielle is my introvert."

They rounded a curve and Sis slowed down. A sign on the edge of the road said Welcome to Stubenville, Population 500.

They weren't going to find much in the way of amenities. Jesse had probably assumed the town was going to be much bigger.

"Where can I drop you folks off at?" Sis asked as she slowed down.

Doubt filled Jesse's voice. "Is there a place we might be able to make a phone call?"

"Not at this hour," Sis said. "You folks look like you could use a shower and some rest. I can drop you off at the Widow Keller's house. She runs an informal bed-and-breakfast," Sis said. "Don't worry about waking her. She's a night owl. Works on her weaving until the wee hours."

"If that's our only option," said Jesse.

Sis eventually pulled up in front of a house.

Abigail and Jesse thanked her. Abigail gave Dawn a poke in the belly. "Thanks for entertaining us, kiddo." The little girl reminded Abigail of her niece, Celeste, her oldest brother's daughter.

"No problem," Dawn chirped, lifting her doll in the air and making it dance.

Jesse and Abigail got out of the car and Sis pulled away from the curb. Dawn waved at them from the back seat. Abigail waved back before turning her attention to the house.

Even in the dark, it looked like something out of a watercolor painting. The porch light was on. Though it was still early spring, tulips and other flowers and greenery bloomed in the garden. Ivy wound around the columns before connecting with the extended roof. The porch swing looked comfortable and inviting.

Under different circumstances, staying here would be a fun adventure. A heaviness invaded Abigail's heart. This wasn't a fun adventure.

"All I have to pay with is a credit card. I'm sure DEA is looking for me to pop up so they have a trace on my card. That means we can't stay here long. Get a quick shower and some sleep. My friend Dale lives about an hour from here. He might be able to help us." Jesse knocked on the door.

A woman with wild white hair that looked like a cloud opened the door. *This must be the Widow Keller.* Jesse explained their situation and apologized for the late hour.

"No problem. I was up, anyway." She ushered them in, Jesse paid for the rooms and the widow pointed up the stairs. "Third and fourth doors on the right. It's a shared bath, but right now you're my only guests. Breakfast is at seven."

"We probably won't be here that long," said Jesse.

"Oh," said the widow as her glance bounced from Jesse to Abigail.

"We just need to get cleaned up and rest a little." Abigail could feel her cheeks getting warm. Did the widow think she and Jesse were a couple?

"Don't need to explain nothing to me. There should be fresh towels in the bath. I could loan you some of my clothes while I toss yours in the wash." She studied Jesse for a moment. "You look like you're about my husband's size. Won't take but an hour to run your clothes through the wash. No extra charge."

Abigail stared down at her muddy clothes. "That would be great."

"I'll leave the clothes outside your doors once they're washed and dried." The widow disappeared down the hallway. "I'll get the fresh ones up to you right away."

They made their way up the stairs. "Why don't you take your shower first?" said Jesse. "When the widow brings the clothes up, I'll set them outside the bathroom door."

Abigail checked several doors before finding the bathroom. Jesse disappeared into one of the rooms they had just paid for.

The bathroom had a deep claw-foot bathtub. A good soak seemed enticing, but she had a feeling time was of the essence. She turned the knobs on the bath and adjusted the temperature. Steam filled up the bathroom almost right away. As the windows steamed up, she pulled back the curtains and stared at the street down below. Light shining from a streetlamp revealed that a car, with a man sitting behind the wheel, was parked across the street.

Her heart beat a little faster. Maybe the man was a local, but in a town this small, it wouldn't be hard to figure out where they were staying. Why would someone sit in their car at night unless they were watching and waiting? The people looking for them could have sent someone to watch the place as soon as they realized they'd escaped.

Jesse was glad to see that there was a phone in his room. The room itself was cozy, with a quilt on the bed and a painting of landscapes on the wall. He picked up the phone and dialed his friend Dale's number.

He touched the hard drive in his pants pocket. Dale, who had computer expertise, would be able to install the drive so he could see exactly what was on it before deciding the best tactic for presenting it to DEA.

Dale picked up the phone after several rings. He sounded out of breath. "Sorry, I was outside. What can I do for you?"

"Dale, this is Jesse Santorum." He and Dale had run operations out of the Southwest, until a bullet to the back put Dale on the disabled list. The man was in chronic pain and walked with a limp.

"Jesse, good to hear from you."

Even though Dale had been forced into retirement, he was still in touch with other active agents. Jesse had to assume Dale might know about the cloud of suspicion that hung over him.

"Have you heard?"

"Yeah, but I knew it wasn't true. I know you," said Dale.

Jesse felt as though a rope that had been wound around his torso had been loosened. Instead of believing the poison Lee had spread in the DEA, Dale knew Jesse's character well enough to know he would never be on the wrong side of the law. "I'm in a bit of a bind, and I'm not far from your neck of the woods."

Jesse gave the short version of all that had happened. Dale promised that he could be in Stubenville in a little over an hour. Jesse said that he and Abigail would be watching for him.

Jesse hung up. He heard a knock on the door and the Widow Keller's voice. "Clothes are just outside the door. You can keep them. Just stuff I don't use anymore. Toss your dirty ones in the hallway."

When Jesse opened the door, the widow was already at the top of the stairs headed down.

"Thanks." Jesse set the blouse and slacks outside the bathroom and picked up the dirty clothes Abigail had tossed outside the door. He could hear the shower running and Abigail singing what sounded like a hymn. No use trying to talk to her above that noise. She'd know to look for the clean clothes.

He took the clothes that were left for him and slumped down in a chair in his room. His eyelids felt heavy. His head bobbed back and then forward. A moment later, he was in a deep sleep…

His eyes shot open.

Abigail stood in front of him looking fresh and clean in a silky-looking royal blue blouse and gray dress pants. Her hair was still wet from the shower.

Seeing her made him smile. "You look nice."

She twirled from side to side. "Thanks."

He glanced around, looking for a clock but not seeing one. He ran his hands through his thick hair. "How long was I out for?"

She shrugged. "I don't know. Maybe half an hour."

"My friend Dale will be here in a little bit. I better get that shower." He jumped up.

"Yes, we should hurry." Her expression had changed. Two deep furrows formed between her eyebrows.

"Something wrong?"

"There's a car parked across the street with a man in it. You can see him from the bathroom window."

That wasn't a surprise, but Jesse tensed up all the same. "Dale will get here as fast as he can." He wished he could do something to ease the fear he saw etched on Abigail's face. He stepped toward her and squeezed her shoulder. "Once I have assurance that you'll be safe, I'll find a way to get you back home."

She slumped down in the chair. "There's not much for me to go back home to…in Fort Madison, anyway." Her eyes were rimmed with tears.

He gathered her into his arms as a desire to protect, to reassure her, surged through him. "We'll get through this. I'm so sorry I got you mixed up in all of this." He stroked the back of her head. "You've handled yourself just fine, Abigail. You're a strong woman."

She rested her head against his chest. "I don't feel very strong right now." She pulled back to look him in the eyes.

He touched her cheek with his thumb. "You are." In that moment, with her looking at him with so much trust in her eyes, he wanted to kiss her. He studied each feature on her face: her slim nose, soft eyes with lush lashes and her cheeks flushed with a rosy glow. Her eyes grew wider and rounder as her lips parted.

He pulled away. It would be wrong to kiss her. "Yeah, you have been stellar. Any other person would have fallen apart. You're cool under fire, Abigail. You'd make a good agent. You ever think about that?"

The words that spilled out of his mouth caught him off guard. Why was he saying such a thing? It sounded like he was trying to find ways to keep being with her when this was all over. Was his connection to her that deep already?

She stepped back, as well. She shook her head and then stared at the floor. The moment of heated intensity between them had been broken. "Guess I never thought about doing anything other than the family business."

He squeezed her shoulder one more time. "I'm going to shower." He stepped out into the hallway, feeling a familiar ache in his chest. The chasm of pain over losing Melissa flooded through him. To love was to risk loss, and he knew he couldn't do that ever again.

He checked the bathroom window before getting in the shower. He saw the car with the driver sitting behind the wheel. He showered and stepped out, wrapping a towel around his waist. When he looked out the window again, the car was gone. That concerned him even more. The window to the bathroom faced a side street. He wondered if the car had moved to the front of the house. He threw his dirty clothes outside the door, taking the hard drive out of his pants pocket. He hadn't put his coat out to be washed. He could put the hard drive back in there.

It could be that whoever was sitting in that car wasn't connected to the drug trade, but he doubted it.

Jesse changed into the overalls and plaid shirt the widow had provided. A sense of urgency told him that maybe it wouldn't be a good idea to hang around here longer than they had to. He glanced at himself in the mirror. Great. He looked like Farmer Brown out to check his crops.

When he stepped into the hallway, his dirty clothes had been picked up. He found Abigail asleep in her room. She looked peaceful, with her hands crossed over her chest and the quilt only half covering her, as if she'd pulled it over herself just as she was falling asleep.

His shower hadn't taken that long. He had maybe another twenty minutes or so before Dale would be here. He left Abigail to get some much-needed rest and hurried downstairs. He stood to the side of the big front window, surveying the street. No sign of the car that had been parked on the side street.

"You gettin' ready to leave so soon?" The widow had come up behind him.

He turned to face her. She was a kind woman. He sure didn't want to put her in any danger. "I have a friend coming to pick us up."

"Be a little while before your clothes are dry," she said.

"Don't worry about it. The clothes you gave us are fine."

She put her hands in the pockets of her apron. "At least let me make a hot cup of tea for you and your friend."

He liked that she didn't ask questions about their strange behavior. Maybe being the only place to stay for miles had taught her to be discreet.

"That would be nice." Jesse settled in a chair that was off to the side, so he had a view of the window without being visible from the street.

The widow brought in a tray with a teapot and two cups.

"This is really wonderful. Thank you." He'd been expecting a tea bag in a mug warmed in the microwave.

"If you're going to have tea, you might as well brew it proper." The widow padded down the hallway, back into a room at the end of the hallway that must be where she did her weaving. Like the hermit and sheepherder, she, too, seemed to lead a solitary life.

Abigail came down the stairs. She held her waterproof jacket. She hadn't put that in the wash.

"Did you get rested?"

He felt an awkwardness between them that hadn't been there before. Had she wanted to kiss him as much as he'd wanted to kiss her? Or was this whole thing one-sided?

"I examined the insides of my eyelids, as my grandpa used to say." She noticed the tray with the pot and teacups. "Wow, what's all this?"

"The widow made us tea. Help yourself." He looked at the clock on the living room wall. "I imagine it'll be a few more minutes before Dale gets here." He slipped into his coat that contained the hard drive.

Abigail poured a cup of the steaming brew, dropped in a sugar cube and sat on the couch.

Jesse stood up and peered out the window again by standing to one side. No new cars had moved into place. "The car that you saw from the bathroom window is gone."

She took a sip of tea. "Maybe it was nothing, then."

He picked up on the tension in her voice. They both knew that someone was looking for them in the area surrounding where the shootout had taken place. It wasn't like there were a hundred small towns they could have gone to.

"I poured you some tea," Abigail said. "Sit down. There's nothing we can do until your friend comes."

She was right. He could pace until there was a hole in the floor and fret all day and night. They would deal with what they had to deal with when and if it happened. For the next few minutes—the time it took to drink a cup of tea—he could catch his breath. He sat down on the couch beside her.

She took a sip of tea. "It's really good."

He plopped in a sugar cube, stirred it with the dainty spoon and brought the steaming cup to his lips. He tasted a mixture of orange and cinnamon. He took several more sips.

Jesse heard footsteps behind him. He had only a second to register that the footfalls were too heavy to be the widow's before he turned to face the barrel of a gun and a grinning face.

Standing beside him, Abigail dropped the teacup

and released an audible breath that sounded like it got choked off in the middle. The echo of the shattering porcelain of the teacup filled the air around him.

NINE

The man sneered, still holding the gun on them. "If the two of you come nice and quiet, nothing will happen to the old lady."

Abigail's heart raced. She gripped Jesse's arm below the elbow. Touching him made her feel less afraid. She sure didn't want anything to happen to the Widow Keller.

"We'll go," said Jesse. "But you have to keep your word about the woman."

"Good, then hurry on out the back door and keep your hands up where I can see them."

Abigail noticed Jesse turning his eyes but not his head toward the front window. Probably checking to see if his friend had made it.

The thug pointed with the gun. He had a scar on his right cheek. His eyes were watery and dark. "Second door on the right. Go out through the kitchen. Don't try anything. I'm right behind you."

Jesse nodded, indicating that Abigail should go ahead of him. They raced past a closed door, where loud instrumental music blared from behind it. Abigail detected the clacking sound of a weaver's loom. The widow wouldn't hear them leaving above all that noise.

They raced through the kitchen. When Abigail stepped outside, another man was waiting for them, leaning against the car they had seen earlier. He held a gun, as well. The two men must have been watching the house through the windows, figuring out how many people were inside.

Jesse glanced around, probably trying to find an escape route. The back alley was dark. They were shielded from view on the street by the neighbor's garage. It was unlikely anyone would be outside at this hour, anyway.

"Get in the back and lie down," said the man with the scar. "Get in now." The guy was clearly nervous and in a hurry to leave before they were spotted.

The car was a sort of caravan with two rows of seats and a back area for hauling larger items—the kind moms used to transport kids and soccer equipment. The kind of car nobody would think was being used for a kidnapping.

Scarface slid open the side door and gestured for Abigail and Jesse to get in.

"Keep your heads down," he said.

Both of them lay on the floor of the van. The two men climbed into the front seats. The van pulled forward and turned. Through the window, she caught flashes of trees and houses bathed in the light from streetlamps. The car gained speed as they got to the edge of the little town.

She turned so she was lying on her side, facing Jesse. She hoped her expression conveyed that she was wondering what they should do. Scarface, who sat in the passenger seat, kept a gun on them.

Jesse shook his head, meaning he didn't have a plan yet. He leaned close to her, so he could whisper in her ear. "They've got to stop sooner or later. That will be our chance."

The heat from his breath lingered on her ear.

"No talking," said the man with the gun in the passenger seat.

The car rumbled down the road.

She prayed the stop would happen before they got to wherever they were being taken. They were being kept alive for some reason. Was it possible the drugs the hermit had taken hadn't been found yet?

In the front seats, the two men were talking. "What is that guy's problem?" said the thug who was driving.

Abigail lifted her head to see what was going on.

Scarface waved his fist in the air. "Yeah, buddy. It's a whole big road here. Why do you got to be right on our tail?" He turned his head to peer out the back window. "Slow down. Maybe he'll pass us."

Abigail lay back down before Scarface could notice her.

The van slowed. She could hear the noise of a car speeding past them. The caravan rolled down the road at a steady pace. Lights flashed in the window. When she raised her head, Abigail saw that they had passed a gas station.

Scarface turned around and waved the gun at her. "Hey, lie down flat."

Were they going to stop at all?

She quelled her fear with a deep breath and a quick prayer.

Jesse reached over and covered her hand with his, as if to reassure her. The warmth of his touch sank into the marrow and she could feel herself calming down.

"Pull over. I need to take a leak," said Scarface.

"Boss said no stopping," said the driver.

Abigail wondered whom they were referencing when they mentioned *the boss*.

"Two minutes. I drank too many energy drinks back there while I was watching the place," said Scarface.

The driver groaned but slowed and pulled over. "Hurry up."

"Okay, Rodney," said Scarface.

Rodney turned in his seat and studied them for a moment before offering them a grin that sent chills down Abigail's spine. "You two look so nice and cozy back there." He lifted his gun, jabbed it in the air and pointed it at them. "No sudden moves." Rodney laughed as he turned around to stare through the windshield. He hit the steering wheel with his palm. "What's taking that guy so long?"

Rodney turned up the radio, so it was blaring.

Once she was sure the driver was not watching them, she lifted her head. With the exception of some bushes where Scarface must have gone, the landscape was flat all around and there was no sign of any dwelling.

If they tried to escape out the back, they'd be shot before they could get to any kind of cover. The gas station they had passed was miles down the road. Rodney was constantly checking his rearview mirror and turning to look at them.

She eased back down and shook her head.

Jesse shrugged his shoulders as if to say he wasn't sure what to do. Rodney turned down the music. He craned his neck one way and then the other, searching. "This is taking too long." He inched the caravan forward and then rolled down the passenger-side window so he could lean across the seat and shout. "Hey,

Larry, come on. We got to get moving!" So Scarface's name was Larry.

Jesse leaped to his feet and placed his arms around Rodney's neck. He yelled at Abigail, "Go!"

Jesse had taken advantage of the moment of distraction.

Heart racing, she struggled to lift the handle on the side door. She could hear the two men fighting. What if Rodney got to his gun and shot Jesse? Larry, the man with a scar, would come back soon enough. She jumped out of the van as she heard the noise of blows being exchanged.

Her feet hit the ground. The sound of the struggle ended. Jesse was close behind her.

The long stretch of open flat road lay to the north and south. The only cover was the bushes, where the other man must have gone. They couldn't go that way.

With Jesse right beside her, she took off at a dead run.

Gunshots boomed behind them. When she glanced over her shoulder, Larry had come out of the bushes and was taking aim at them.

The second gunshot was so loud she felt like her eardrums had been punctured. Jesse veered toward the side of the road. Smart move. Though there was no place to take cover, getting away from the road and running into the darkness would make them harder to hit.

She saw headlights in the distance looming toward them. Another vehicle.

Please, God, let this be someone who is willing to stop.

Larry continued to run toward them, stopping to fire off another round.

She stuttered in her steps, unwilling to give in to the terror that gripped her. Jesse spurted ahead of her, running parallel to the road as the headlights of the on-coming car drew near.

She heard the sound of the van starting up. Rodney must have come to. They'd have no chance at all once he got the van turned around. They had to get off the road or be run down.

The oncoming four-wheel drive braked on the shoulder some thirty feet away. His stop was so sudden that his tires spit gravel. The driver rolled down his window and stuck his head out, waving at them.

"That's Dale." Jesse ran faster.

Behind them, the van had been turned around and the driver rolled out onto the road, gaining speed as Larry, still on foot, closed the distance between them.

Dale pulled back out on the road and sped toward them. He stopped in the middle of the road. Jesse fumbled with the back door.

Another shot was fired.

Jesse swung open the door, stepped to one side so Abigail could get in first and then fell in himself while Dale shifted into Reverse, pressed the gas, cranked the steering wheel and spun around his car.

Abigail stared out the back window. The driver had stopped long enough for the passenger to hop into the van before speeding toward Dale's four-wheel drive. The delay bought them precious seconds.

"Let's see if we can lose these guys." Dale glanced in the rearview mirror.

Jesse finally succeeded in closing the back door. He pressed his back against the seat and stared at the ceiling.

"Abigail, this is my friend Dale," Jesse said, out of breath from running.

"Pleased to meet you." Dale never took his eyes off

the road. "Looks like we got a job on our hands here, Jesse." Dale's voice was infused with affection. The two men must have some sort of history together. Dale increased his speed and then turned off the paved road onto a dirt one. "Nothing I can't handle."

"Pleased to meet you, too." Abigail was still recovering from the adrenaline rush of getting away from the guys in the van.

The dirt road got bumpier. The van stayed close behind them.

Dale leaned forward. "Get your seat belts on. This is going to get way worse before it gets better."

The four-wheel drive bounced and swayed on the rough road.

Looking into Jesse's eyes calmed her. The vehicle jerked wildly, and both of them jolted around as they fumbled to secure the seat belts.

"Keep 'er steady there, Dale." Jesse's tone was light-hearted, almost joking.

"I'm doing my best, friend," said Dale.

She wasn't sure how the two men could joke around with the van still bearing down on them and the condition of the road getting worse, but she would take the levity over the white-knuckle terror that she was fighting not to give in to.

Just then, Dale's four-wheel drive hit a bump.

Dale checked his rearview mirror. "Now that you two are buckled up, things are going to get really interesting."

Abigail glanced through the rear window. The van had closed the distance between them.

Dale sped up and turned off the road toward a cluster of trees. "Don't worry," said Dale. "There is a road here...sort of." Dale laughed.

Abigail was starting to wonder if she was in a vehicle with a crazy man. She shot Jesse a raised eyebrow and shook her head.

"Dale gets a thrill out of four-wheelin', is all," Jesse said. His voice gave away how exciting it was for him, too. Some men thrived on danger.

"It's even more fun when you're being chased. Remember that time in Colombia?"

"Yeah, I remember. That Jeep was so old and rusted out, you could look through the floor at the scenery." Jesse turned slightly toward Abigail. "Dale and I used to run operations together."

"So I gathered." The camaraderie between the two men was neat to witness.

Dale continued to aim toward the trees. As they got closer, she saw no sign of a road.

Dale drove through the trees and out onto ground that was rockier. His four-wheel drive was able to crawl over boulders. The headlights of the van grew farther away and then disappeared altogether. Finally, he pulled out onto what looked like a country road. She was grateful that they'd stopped jerking around as Dale increased his speed and took them up a winding road, where the trees were more abundant.

The path they were on smoothed out. They weren't being jostled from side to side as much. She couldn't see the van at all now.

Abigail closed her eyes and took in a deep breath. They were safe…for now.

Dale brought his four-wheel drive to a stop outside a cabin that was partially hidden from view by evergreens. Though he had heard about it from other agents, Jesse had never been to Dale's secluded retirement home. He pushed open his own door and hurried around to Abigail's side. Once again, she'd handled herself like a champion.

Jesse held the door for Abigail while she slid out and looked around. Dale was already headed up the trail toward the cabin.

Dale yelled over his shoulder, "Both of you can grab a couple of logs on your way in. I'll get a fire started."

Abigail glanced around. "This looks really primitive... and far away from everything."

Jesse rested his hand on her shoulder. "I'm sure Dale has made the place very livable."

Abigail made her way up the trail, where flat rocks had been pressed into the dirt to create a path.

Once they were on the cabin's porch, Jesse said, "Hold your hands out in front of you. I'll load you up with logs."

Abigail obliged and Jesse placed several logs in her C-shaped arms. "Let me know when it's heavy enough for you."

"I'm starting to see a theme here." Abigail turned slightly toward the cabin door.

"What do you mean?"

"Dale is another isolated loner. Like the hermit and Edward and even that widow."

"Some people just choose to be alone for whatever reason." Dale hadn't always lived alone. A painful divorce shortly before he retired had left the man disillusioned. "Dale has two grown sons who come out here all the time. He's in touch with lots of agents still in the field. Sometimes pain drives your life in a particular direction." He understood that more than anyone.

"I know. After Brent, I thought about going up in the mountains just living by myself, but you have to go on, right? You have to find some way to heal." She looked off in the distance. "I have to figure out what my life is going to look like without him and the plans we made together."

"Right." Jesse picked up several logs until his own arms were full. As he watched Abigail disappear inside the cabin, it occurred to him that it was possible to be living in a city and still be living in isolation. It was what he had done since Melissa's death.

He checked the surrounding woods for any signs of movement and listened for a moment. Confident that they had not been followed, he stepped inside. The cabin was one large room with a loft. One corner was dedicated to computers and computer parts, and another contained a refrigerator and stove. On the other side of the room, Dale had already started a fire in the fireplace. Jesse dumped his firewood and plopped down on a worn leather couch that faced the fire.

He pulled the hard drive he'd been hauling around out of his pocket. "Can we get this installed and see what's on it?" Jesse still didn't have a clear plan as to whom he could trust with the information on the drive. It occurred to him that he might get it into the hands of one of the other agents who knew him, and then it could be passed up the line to the supervisors who thought he was the turncoat.

Dale threw another log on the fire. "Hold your horses now. We got time and I don't often get company."

"What about the guys in the van?"

"We'll keep watch for them. But that van they were

driving won't handle as well on these roads as my vehicle." said Dale.

Abigail turned toward the kitchen area. "I could make some tea."

"That sounds like a great idea," said Dale.

The fire crackled as flames shot up and grew larger.

Dale sat opposite Jesse in an overstuffed chair that looked like something Dale might have picked up out of a dumpster or off the curb. It was made of some sort of orange velvet material. A stack of books sat beside it, so Dale must use it as his reading chair.

Dale leaned forward and held out his hand. "Let me see what you got there."

Jesse handed him the hard drive.

Dale turned it over in his hands. "Oh, yeah, this is all just standard stuff. Shouldn't be too much trouble at all."

The kettle whistled, and a moment later, Abigail brought them each a cup of tea and then returned to get one for herself. She sat down on the couch a few feet from Jesse. After several sips of tea, Jesse could feel himself relaxing. It was still dark outside. The sun would be coming up shortly.

Dale asked Abigail several questions about where she was from and what she did for a living.

"And how did you get tangled up with this guy?" Dale sat back in his chair.

Abigail gazed over at Jesse. "That's a long story."

He thought he saw affection in her eyes. Of course, after all they had been through, they felt a bond toward each other. But was he sensing even deeper feelings?

"Once I'm sure she's not going to be a target, I need to see she gets home safely," said Jesse.

Abigail circled the rim of the mug with her finger

and stared into her tea. "Yes, all of this has been very exciting, but I suppose I need to go back...home."

He picked up on the pain in her voice.

Dale and Jesse talked and joked some about some of the investigations they had worked together on, and then Dale retreated to his worktable with the hard drive. "There's sandwich stuff in the fridge if you two are hungry," Dale called from across the room.

Jesse covered Abigail's hand with his. "Let me get it. You got the tea."

Abigail jumped to her feet. "I'll help you. It's not like I have something else to do."

Jesse pulled cold cuts, cheese and condiments from the refrigerator while Abigail searched the cupboards for bread.

They made the sandwiches and sat back down in front of the fire.

After he took several bites, Jesse watched the fire and contemplated the next steps he needed to take. "Abigail, I may have to travel to another state to get this information to someone who can help me. I'm concerned that if you go back to Fort Madison, you will still be a target."

Abigail straightened her spine. "I was thinking I should just go back to Idaho, where my family is. There's nothing left for me in Fort Madison other than to get my stuff and offer my employer an explanation. I can wait on getting my stuff."

"That might be safer," Jesse said.

"You don't sound so sure."

The cartel could find out easily enough where her family lived. Maybe she would be safer if she stayed here with Dale until he could clear his name and get her some protection. He wasn't sure what to do. All he knew was that the thought of being separated from her made him uneasy…and sad.

Dale pushed his rolling chair back from his worktable. "All right, folks, I think I got this thing installed and ready to run."

Jesse took in a breath. This was it. The moment of truth. Everything he'd been fighting for since he'd walked into the office of Big Sky Outfitters.

A million questions bombarded his brain as he walked across the wood floor toward the wall of computers. Would what was on the hard drive be enough to exonerate him? Would he be able to get it to someone who could help clear his name?

TEN

As they walked across the floor, Abigail felt as though she and Jesse were once again coming to the end of their need to stay together. A heaviness like a lead blanket weighed on her shoulders. The revelation that there was nothing for her in Fort Madison left a big hole inside her. Sure, she could go back to her family in Idaho. She could go back to working as a guide where she'd grown up. But was that what she wanted?

The laptop screen in front of Dale glowed, and then icons that indicated files came on the screen.

Jesse rested his hand on the back of Dale's chair and leaned closer to the screen. "So it looks like the first three are audio files." He pointed at one of the icons. "That must be the file that contains the undoctored photos. I'm not sure what this last file is that only has numbers for a title. Open up the photo file and let me see what's there."

"I'll let you have a look," said Dale, rising from his chair. "I'm going to grab a sandwich for myself."

After Jesse took over Dale's seat, Abigail edged closer, peering over Jesse's shoulder as he scrolled through photographs. The only thing the images had in common was a man with a buzz cut. The pictures showed him entering an airport holding a briefcase, sitting at a table with men who had tattoos on their necks and arms, standing outside a bar with a Spanish name. And sitting at a restaurant with men in business suits.

"Is that Lee? The man who set you up?"

Jesse nodded. "Yes, that's him. The doctored photos the DEA got had me doing all this stuff. Part of me just doesn't want to believe Lee would do such a thing."

Jesse clicked on the file that only had numbers for a title. A video of Lee came on-screen as he adjusted the camera and sat back. Lee's shoulders drooped, and he had dark circles under his eyes. Though it was dimly lit, it was clear the recording had been done inside the airplane that had been landed in the mountains outside Fort Madison.

"If you have found this file, it means I'm dead. Nobody knows I kept the original files but me. I was told to destroy them. I never meant for this to go as far as it did. I didn't want to make Agent Santorum take the fall. He's a good guy. Emily had medical bills we couldn't pay, and this was a way to make some cash on the side."

Jesse drummed on the table with his fingers. His jaw was set tight. What he was hearing was upsetting him. Abigail spoke in a soft voice. "Who was Emily?"

Jesse ran his hands through his hair. "His daughter. She had some sort of chronic illness."

Lee continued to talk on the screen. "When I tried to get out, I couldn't. Taking this plane was my insurance. A way to get the upper hand. No one knows where it is but me."

All the color drained from Jesse's face as he hit the pause button on the video. "It sounds like someone else was calling the shots on this whole working-with-the-cartel thing, and Lee was just a go-between."

Dale stood behind them holding his sandwich. "Another agent maybe?"

Jesse rubbed his chin. "Lee seemed afraid in Mexico, even before we got in that firefight. Maybe the dirty agent was there with us." Jesse's voice took on a faraway quality. He stared at the wall as though he was rerunning the events of that night. "Maybe he was going to tell me who it was…and he just ran out of time."

Jesse hit the play button on the video. Lee rested his head in his hands for a moment before looking at the camera again. His eyes were glazed with weariness and defeat. "Agent Frisk has been working with the drug dealers, feeding them information, helping them move product, giving them warnings for over a year now. He's the one who had me frame Jesse."

The screen went black.

Jesse sat back in the chair. "Agent Frisk was there the night Lee died." Jesse closed his eyes and massaged the area between his eyebrows. "When I think about the way things played out, Lee might not have been shot by the dealers. It might have been Frisk who shot him."

"Maybe Frisk figured out Lee was getting cold feet."

"Maybe." Jesse's jawline hardened. He bolted up from the chair. Turning his back toward Abigail and Dale, he took several steps, placed his hands on his hips and shook his head. The stiffness through his shoulders indicated how upset he was.

A tense quiet overtook the room. Abigail's heart lurched. Jesse was dealing with so much right now. She wasn't sure what to say.

The window Abigail stood by shattered. Broken glass

came at her like a thousand tiny knifes. Instinctually, Abigail fell to the floor and crawled toward the shelter of the computer worktable. Her heart raced as the adrenaline kicked in.

Dale scrambled across the floor on all fours. "Looks like they found us."

Jesse dived for cover by the couch.

Dale opened a table by the couch, pulled out a handgun and slid it toward Jesse. He crawled around toward a gun rack over the fireplace and retrieved a rifle.

Abigail braced for more gunshots. Shards of glass in various sizes were strewed across the floor.

"Abigail, get the laptop." Jesse pointed at the worktable.

Even as her heart pounded wildly, a curious calm washed over her. They needed to save that hard drive. She reached up and felt around for the edge of the laptop, then pulled it down toward her.

Dale made his way toward the shattered window. "If you can get to that screwdriver and pull the hard drive, that would be good."

Crouching beneath the height of the window, she moved across the floor toward where a screwdriver had rolled off the table. She returned to the safety that the underside of the worktable provided. She shut off the laptop and then flipped it over.

Dale peered above the rim of the broken window while Jesse checked out the window that faced the front of the cabin.

"See anything?" Jesse crouched beneath the window with his gun drawn.

Dale shook his head. "You?"

Jesse lifted his head again above the rim of the

window. "Some movement in the trees. They're repositioning. Can't tell how many. Don't see a vehicle. They must have parked a ways away."

As she loosened the screws on the bottom of the laptop, her fingers remained steady despite her rapid pulse. It was as if some instinct had taken over. She'd felt this before when encountering animals in the wild. It was as if her body overrode whatever fear her mind was battling. Her legs knew whether the smart thing to do was to run or stand still. She felt the same thing now, even though Dale's cabin was under siege.

She opened the laptop and pulled out the hard drive, placing it in her pocket. They were in this fight together. Jesse was a good man. She wanted to help him clear his name. "Dale, you got a gun for me?"

Dale had worked his way over to the only other window by the kitchen area. "You know how to use it?"

"Yes, she does," said Jesse. Admiration colored his words as he gazed at her.

Dale pointed to a bookcase on Jesse's side of the room. "Behind *The History of Rome*."

Abigail got to the bookcase just as another shot was fired through the broken window. The bullet ricocheted off something solid, making a pinging noise. Dale returned fire, then rested his rifle on the rim of the broken window and looked through his scope. He shot two rounds before dipping below the window frame.

"Can you see them out there?" Jesse worked his way to Dale.

"I didn't see anyone, but I can tell you where the shot came from," said Dale.

Abigail pulled the heavy volume off the bookshelf, where a handgun with a short barrel was hidden. She flipped open the cylinder. The gun was a revolver with six bullets. "What do you think they're trying to do?"

"Flush us out into the open," said Jesse. "Who knows, there might just be one guy out there."

"Tell you what," said Dale. "How about I hold them or him off while you two get to my vehicle? I have another car stored deeper in the forest."

Judging from all the guns he had hidden and the second car, Dale seemed to have all sorts of contingency plans for survival and escape. Maybe agents always worried that people they had put in jail might come after them when they got out. And maybe they just learned to always have a backup plan.

"Are you sure about that?" Jesse glanced in Abigail's direction and then looked back at Dale. "That's a big risk."

"Won't be my first time in a firefight," said Dale. "I kind of miss it sometimes. Toss me your gun. I can make it sound like there are ten of us in here. You and Abigail take the little snub-nosed pistol. The keys for the four-wheel drive are in that bowl on the table by the door."

"Will do." Jesse nodded at his friend. "Thanks for everything, Dale." He hurried across the floor toward Abigail, who had already retrieved the keys from the bowl.

Behind her, Dale started to fire shots, first from the rifle and then from the handgun. The shots came so fast they almost seemed to overlap. Jesse grabbed Abigail's hand and squeezed it before reaching for the door handle.

Taking in a breath and drawing strength from Jesse holding her hand, Abigail braced herself, ready to step out into what might be a hail of gunfire.

* * *

"Be as quiet as possible," Jesse whispered. He pushed the door open so there was a narrow slit for him and Abigail to slip through. He went first, regretting that he had to let go of Abigail's hand.

Their feet made soft padding noises as they moved across the porch. Jesse surveyed the surrounding trees for movement or the flash of a gunshot. From inside the house, they could hear the rapid exchange of fire between Dale and whoever was at the back of the house. The gunfire would cease for several seconds and then resume. Dale must have dug up more bullets at some point.

Jesse took in a deep breath. "Let's make a run for it."

They sprinted down the steps toward Dale's four-wheel drive.

The silence made him that much more vigilant. He slipped behind the steering wheel, and Abigail handed him the keys. He turned the key in the ignition.

The gunfire on the far side of the house stopped.

Jesse shifted into Reverse and turned around. "Stay down. We don't know what kind of numbers we're dealing with here." He assumed it was only the two men who had taken them from the bed-and-breakfast, but it was dangerous to assume.

Abigail put her head on the seat.

A gunshot came at them from behind. In his rearview mirror, Jesse watched a man shooting from the side of the house, barely visible in the early-morning light.

He hit the gas and headed toward the winding trail. When he checked the rearview mirror one more time, he saw that Dale had come around the back of the shooter and overtaken him. The shooter looked like the one called Rodney. Dale would be okay and would probably get Rodney turned in to the sheriff to deal with after he questioned him. The thug might have useful information.

Jesse sped down the winding road. The glint of metal caught his eye up ahead. The thugs' van was parked to one side of the road, facing downhill for a quick escape. They must have seen the smoke from the cabin fire and known that it was just around the bend. When he drove past, there was no one behind the wheel. He saw no movement in the surrounding area, either. Both men must have gone up to the cabin.

Jesse stopped, but left the vehicle running. "Just a second. Let me make sure that other guy doesn't get off the mountain." He took the gun and walked toward the parked van, prepared to blow out the tires.

Just as he drew the gun up and placed his finger on the trigger, the engine of Dale's four-wheel drive revved up. At first, he thought Abigail had slipped over into the driver's seat to move the car for whatever reason, but then he saw the thug called Larry behind the wheel, driving away with Abigail. He must have been hiding in the trees or going to the bathroom again.

Jesse swung open the driver's-side door of the van and hopped in. He was grateful to see the keys had been tossed into the console. His heart squeezed tight as he fired up the van and pulled out, prepared to chase Larry and Abigail.

He watched the taillights of Dale's vehicle disappear around a corner. It was moving so fast it seemed to catch air as it turned. The van handled poorly on the rough roads. He fought off that feeling of helplessness—the same feeling he'd had when Melissa had first been diagnosed with cancer.

Abigail wasn't going to die. Not on his watch.

He said a quick prayer for Abigail's safety and pressed down on the gas.

ELEVEN

All the air left Abigail's lungs as her whole body tensed.

The driver, Larry, spoke through gritted teeth. "Don't try anything, lady." He drove one-handed and held his gun close to his stomach, pointed at her.

She glanced through the back window but saw only the empty winding road behind her as they rounded a curve.

"Don't you want to wait for your friend?"

"He wasn't my friend. I know what happened to him. That guy in the cabin has him. That's why I hightailed it back down to the van before he took me out, too. Running into you makes my life that much easier."

The man seemed extremely agitated. He kept re-adjusting the grip of the gun in his hand.

Was there some way she could get the upper hand psychologically? She was used to dealing with wild animals. They had predictable patterns of behavior. "It doesn't matter what happened to your partner? What was his name? Rodney?"

The man kept his eyes on the road, but his whole body stiffened. "If I don't bring you two in, I'm in big trouble. That's all I know."

The words sank in just as she turned slightly to see Jesse following in the van. So the plan must be to use her as bait to lure Jesse to wherever he needed to be taken. Of course, Jesse would come after them to try to get her free.

Her hand touched the hard drive in her pocket. She hadn't had a chance to give it back to Jesse.

The driver made his way down the winding road and out onto a two-lane highway. The terrain became flat again, allowing her to see for miles. In the distance, she saw bundles of light scattered all over the landscape with one large concentration of lights. That had to be the Bakken oil fields and whatever boomtown was close to it.

Larry continued to talk. "There's a phone in my shirt pocket. Take it out. Dial the number for Ernie and tell him I'm headed toward the Tasco truck stop. We're about ten minutes away." The driver shot her a look. "And don't try anything."

She pulled out the phone, wondering if by making this phone call, she was signing her and Jesse's death warrants. She scrolled through the list of phone numbers until she found the one that said Ernie and pressed the icon to dial.

"Yes." The voice on the other end of the line came across harsh and demanding.

Abigail cleared her throat. "I'm supposed to tell you that we're headed toward the Tasco truck stop. We'll be there in ten minutes."

"Tell him target one is in the van and that I have target two in a rust-colored four-wheel drive," said Larry. "Tell him Rodney is out of the game."

It seemed a bit cavalier to say someone was out of the

game when they had been captured by Dale and would probably be turned over to the law. But she gripped the phone and repeated what Larry told her.

"Too bad about Rodney. That might come back to bite us down the line if he squawks." The voice on the phone grunted. "I can send someone to the truck stop about the same time you get there." Ernie disconnected. She doubted that was the man's real name. When she'd scrolled through the contacts, she'd noticed other names from children's programs listed. They probably all had code names on the phones.

She put down the phone and repeated what the voice had told her.

Larry seemed to calm down a little. His shoulders weren't as stiff. "Good, this is all going to turn out okay."

Abigail didn't feel any less afraid. Maybe things would turn out okay for Larry, but what about them?

She saw the lights of the truck stop up ahead. Jesse continued to follow them in the van. The truck stop was humming with activity. Larry hit his blinker and pulled off. He rolled through the truck stop, past the gas pumps and the structure that housed a café and casino. He headed toward a corner of the property that was away from all the activity.

Abigail glanced over her shoulder but didn't see any other headlights. Where had Jesse gone? Maybe he realized this was a trap and was trying to come up with a sneakier plan to get her free. She knew Jesse well enough by now to know that he wouldn't give up without a fight.

The driver brought the car to a stop and turned off

all the lights. He lifted the gun, pointing it at her head. "Don't even twitch a muscle."

Abigail sat still, but looked around Dale's car and outside by moving her eyes but not her neck.

Larry shifted in his seat. "What's taking them so long?"

Out of the corner of her eye, she saw the headlights of the van as it parked some distance away and Jesse got out, sneaking into the bushes. She shifted forward slightly to block Larry's view.

"I said don't move."

"Sorry, I'm just very uncomfortable," she said.

In her periphery vision, she watched as another car pulled up to the van. Two men got out and ran toward where Jesse was hiding. Her breath caught. Those men were after Jesse.

"Something wrong?" Larry rubbed the scar on his face.

"No, I just…" She knew she had to get away to help Jesse. She turned suddenly and punched Larry hard in the neck. Stunned, he wheezed for breath and loosened his grip on the gun. She pushed the door open and leaped out, landing hard on the gravel. She pulled herself to her feet and took off running. The car that pulled up by the van was driving away—probably with Jesse inside.

Jesse was lying in the back seat of a car with a hood over his head. The car started rolling but never gained speed. They must still be in the truck-stop parking lot. The ambush had caught him off guard. He'd been focused on his own surprise assault on the car where Abigail was.

Of course, he knew it might be a setup to get to him. Why else would the guy park and wait? But he had done a circuitous route through the truck-stop parking lot to make sure he wasn't followed.

The car stopped. Hands gripped and lifted him. Still unable to see, he struggled to break free, flailing his arms. Despite not being able to see, he landed one solid punch before a Taser made him writhe and recoil, then bend forward at the waist. He felt nauseous from the Taser blast.

He heard a door swing open, and then a voice commanded, "Get up those stairs. Two of them."

He was pushed forward and then someone put hands on his shoulders and directed him down onto a chair. The room smelled musty, like old shoes.

He stood to put up a fight, reaching to take the hood off his head.

He heard the slide of a gun whiz back and forth as a bullet slipped into the chamber. "Don't even try," said a voice.

He sat back down. Someone grabbed his hands and tied them so his wrists were bound in front of him. The hood was yanked off his head. He blinked, waiting for his eyes to adjust to the dimness of the room.

When he'd driven into the truck-stop parking lot, he'd noticed four or five run-down trailers on the far end of the multiacre property. His best guess was that he was being held in one of those trailers. The trailers were probably cheap sleeping quarters for the workers headed toward the Bakken oil fields. Though this one clearly had not been used for a long time. The wind blew through it, causing the metal to rattle. A rusty sink attached to the wall dripped water. He thought he saw a mattress in a dark corner.

He was seated on a lumpy recliner. Across from him sat a man in the shadows on a dining chair. The man with the gun stood off to one side.

The man in the shadows got up and walked toward him. Jesse recognized him as the dark-haired man from the mountain.

He leaned very close to Jesse and grinned, revealing a gold-capped tooth. He pulled back and paced. "Agent Santorum. We have a few questions to ask you, but first, stand up and let my associate search you."

The second man handed the gun to the dark-haired man and then patted Jesse down.

"There's nothing on him," said the associate.

The dark-haired man handed the gun back to his associate. "Have a seat, Agent Santorum."

Jesse hesitated. The associate poked the gun in his direction. Jesse sat back down.

The dark-haired man crossed his arms over his chest. "It seems we ran into a very strange old man up in those mountains."

"You didn't hurt him, did you?"

The dark-haired man let out a huff of air. "Relax, your little hermit pal is fine. Besides, who is he going to talk to and who's going to believe him? Turns out he was quite the negotiator in terms of us getting our product back."

Jesse had a feeling he knew where the story was leading. He wasn't about to give anything away.

"With some persuading, he mentioned that you showed a keen interest in what he called a little black box, which sounds a great deal like a hard drive. What was on that hard drive and where did you put it?"

So this was why he and Abigail had not been killed outright. They hadn't been searched by the men who found them at Abigail's trailer. Somewhere between that time and now, the other men must have run into the hermit on the mountain. The men who took them at the bed-and-breakfast had been in a rush. At first, they had been kept alive to give up where the missing product had gone. Even if these men didn't know exactly what was on the hard drive, they knew it was important and that they needed to get the hard drive back before it fell into the wrong hands. "I don't know what you're talking about."

The man with the gun leaned over and hit Jesse hard across the jaw. Jesse sat up straight, still stinging from the blow. He tasted blood in his mouth. Raising his head, he narrowed his eyes at the dark-haired man. "I still don't know what you're talking about." He'd been tortured before. He wasn't about to say that Abigail had the hard drive.

He wondered, too, if Agent Frisk was calling the shots behind all of this. If so, he seemed to have access to a lot of manpower.

The dark-haired man studied him for a long moment before nodding at his associate, who proceeded to hit Jesse in the face and stomach. Jesse doubled over as his stomach churned and his eyes watered from the blow to the face.

A long tense moment passed before the dark-haired man spoke. "Still not talking. We'll see how you feel about that after a little bit." The dark-haired man scooted his chair across the floor, making a high-pitched screeching noise.

Both men lunged for Jesse. Jesse twisted, trying to fight free. The associate pulled out a hypodermic and plunged it into Jesse's arm. He could feel the poison traveling through his veins instantly. His mind fogged and his body grew weak as one of the men stood on the chair and the other restrained Jesse.

Now he saw what they were going to do. A beam ran all the way across the ceiling of the trailer. Together the two men strung him up, so he was hanging with his arms above him and standing on tiptoe.

He was familiar with this interrogation technique. The physical and emotional strain was intended to break him down. They'd return in a few hours and promise him food and release in exchange for answers about the hard drive. He wasn't about to give in.

The drug he'd been given was clearly designed to leave him in a weakened state. His muscles became leaden, and maybe the drug would even knock him out. He didn't know. He was having a hard time thinking clearly. His vision blurred, and he felt like he was watching the two men through a window smeared with petroleum jelly as they left the trailer. The door closed with a screech.

Jesse squeezed his eyes shut and opened them several times, trying to make his mind work. His arm muscles strained from being stretched above him. He was able to turn in a half circle one way and then the other. Nothing that might help him escape was within reach.

His eyelids were so heavy, and his brain felt as though it had been stuffed with cotton.

His mind wandered to Abigail. Had they captured

her, too? Once they found the hard drive, they would dispose of her. The thought of any harm coming to Abigail helped him find his strength and resolve. He had to get out of here. Somehow. Some way.

Again, he turned in a half circle one way and then the other. He saw the gleam of metal along the wall. Some kind of tool maybe.

How was he going to get out of here and find Abigail?

TWELVE

Abigail ran toward the bright lights of the truck stop.
It would be only a matter of seconds before Larry got
his bearings and came after her. She'd seen where the
car that held Jesse had turned, disappearing behind
some trailers that looked like they were no longer used
on the edge of the property opposite where Larry had
taken her.

She knew she had to get to Jesse to help him, but
right now she needed to go toward the safety of people,
where Larry could not come after her. She was no good
to Jesse if she got caught, too.

She willed her legs to move faster. When she looked
over her shoulder, Larry had turned the four-wheel drive
around and was driving toward her. Outside the truck
stop, there were several cars parked but no people.

She ran faster even as she felt the four-wheel drive
bearing down on her.

She could see the bright lights of the café, where
several people sat in booths and a waitress scurried
across the floor with a tray. None of them looked up
or noticed her.

It felt like the car was right behind her.

A man with a potbelly wearing a baseball hat stepped out of the casino and paced the sidewalk. He looked directly at her. Something in his expression changed when he looked at her.

She glanced over her shoulder.

Larry was still headed toward the truck stop.

Her feet touched the edge of the sidewalk.

The man in the baseball hat turned toward her. His gaze went to where Larry rolled toward the sidewalk and then back to her. "Hey there, little lady. Looks like you're in some kind of trouble."

She wasn't sure if the man in the baseball hat was any safer than the one who had just tried to run her down, but she sure was glad he'd stepped outside when he did.

She pressed her palm against her chest where her heart was raging from exertion. "I'll be all right, thank you."

She hurried inside the café and took a booth that gave her a view of the edge of the property, where Jesse was probably being kept. The waitress came over to her and put down a menu.

"Can I get you anything to drink for a start?"

Disoriented, Abigail stared up at the older woman, who had a kind face. She maybe had a few dollars in her jacket pocket. "Can I just get a cup of coffee?"

"Sure, honey, no problem."

Larry eased forward in the four-wheel drive, parking right by the window where she was sitting. Even through the glass, she could see the menacing look on his face. If she left the café, he would come after her.

The waitress brought her a beige coffee cup.

"Have you decided what you want to eat?"

Abigail stared at the steam rising out of the mug. Her

heart still hadn't slowed down. What was she going to do? How could she get to Jesse? What if they had plans to move him or kill him?

Her throat tightened. What if they had killed him already?

The waitress turned, took two steps away from her table and then whirled back around. "Are you okay? You seem…afraid."

Abigail gazed at the older woman. Her name tag said Mary. "I am afraid. You see that man parked in that car out there? He's stalking me. If I leave the café, he'll come after me."

Mary took a moment to answer. She placed a fist on her hip. "You poor thing. That's not right. I'm sure it will be no problem for me to give highway patrol a buzz, and they can question or hold him or whatever they do to make sure you can leave. And don't worry about that coffee. I'll cover it."

Abigail turned her head to look out the window. Off in the distance, she could see where Jesse had parked the van. "Thank you. I just want to get to my car and drive away without him following me."

"I don't know how all that works, but I'm sure I can call the highway patrol and let them know what's going on. Since this is the only truck stop for miles, they usually get here pretty quick."

She watched Mary walk away and disappear behind the swinging doors that led to the kitchen.

Her fingers were trembling as she opened the sugar packet and poured it into the coffee. She sipped the hot beverage.

Her gaze went from Larry in the car to the trailers to the long stretch of property that led out to the highway.

Her coffee was nearly gone when the highway patrol car pulled into the huge lot. She saw the shocked look on Larry's face as it rolled through the parking lot toward him. Larry started Dale's four-wheel drive and backed out of his space, pulling away and gaining speed with the highway patrol on his bumper.

Now was her chance. She hurried out of the café and jogged toward the van. She was out of breath by the time she made it across the huge lot. Her fingers touched the door handle and she clicked it open. Her spirits lifted. Jesse had left the keys in the ignition. She hopped into the driver's seat and rolled across the parking lot.

The place where the trailers were was in the far corner of the truck stop, an area that was not paved, just gravel. The bright lights of the café and gas pumps did not reach to this dark corner. She parked a short way away and then hurried toward the trailers. There were four trailers in all. She pressed her back against the first one, which had a door that hung crookedly. She rolled along the metal side of the trailer to peek inside—empty except for some broken furniture. Crouching, she hurried to the second trailer. Voices drifted out of an opening where a door used to be. It sounded like two men were playing cards and joking.

She made her way to the area between the second and third trailers, where the car that had taken Jesse was parked. She sprinted to the far side of the third trailer and swung the door open. Her breath caught when she saw Jesse strung up from the rafters. His head wobbled on his neck. He looked at her with glazed eyes. "Hey." Even in his drugged state, his face lit up when he saw her. "You found me."

"'Course I found you. We're in this together, right?"
Her heart lurched. What kind of pain had he endured?

"Got to hand it to you, Abigail. I'm impressed with
your skills."

She pulled her knife from her pocket and pushed the
chair toward him. "We're going to get you down from
here." She sawed back and forth on the rope until it
broke. Jesse's arms fell to his side and his knees buckled, though he remained on his feet.

She reached toward him to steady him.

"I can make it," he said, pulling away from her. He
tried to stand on his own but swayed.

She caught him. "We don't have much time."

"They want the hard drive. I'm glad you had it.
Otherwise they would have killed me and taken it."

She didn't even want to think about Jesse dying. "We
better get moving." She helped him down the stairs.
"The van is parked a little ways away. I didn't want
them to hear it." She still had her arm around his back,
her hand resting on her shoulder. They stepped outside.

They were within five yards of the van when she
heard the thugs' car start up. She took the few steps
to the van, still supporting Jesse. She swung open the
passenger-side door. With some effort, Jesse pulled himself up into the seat while she got behind the steering
wheel.

The thugs' car was headed straight toward them.

When she turned the key in the ignition, the van
sputtered and then started. "We're almost out of gas."

Jesse laughed. "We're at a gas station." He was still
a little out of it from the drugs.

She pressed the accelerator and headed toward the

lights of the truck stop, knowing they would be safe once they were around people.

The thugs' bumper hit the back of the van, jarring her in the seat.

Steeling herself, she gripped the steering wheel and drove toward one of the gas pumps.

Jesse pulled his credit card from his pocket. "Pay with this."

While she pumped the gas, the thugs stopped their car and got out. One of them leaned against the hood and crossed his arms while the other stood with his hands on his hips so the top of his gun was visible beneath his coat. She recognized the dark-haired man from the mountain.

Despite being a little unsure on his feet, Jesse got out of the van and stood beside her. He rested a supportive palm on her shoulder.

She glanced over at the two thugs as she struggled to get a deep breath because of the panic she felt. "How are we going to get out of here? They'll follow us for sure."

Both directions were miles and miles of rural roads, with only tiny towns dotting the landscape. There might not even be that much.

"I need time for this drug to wear off, and we need to find a safe hiding place for that hard drive. They got their drugs back. That's why they didn't kill us outright. If they find the hard drive on us, we're dead."

His words sent a new wave of fear through her. She finished pumping the gas. The man in Dale's four-wheel drive, Larry, had parked away from the truck stop. The highway patrol must have not been able to detain him as long as it took to question him.

"Jesse, what do we do?"

"Let's go inside the truck stop and sit until we can figure something out," Jesse said. "I need this brain fog to go away before we try anything."

With the men still watching them, Abigail got behind the wheel and pulled the van closer to the truck stop. She felt the weight of the hard drive against her stomach in her pocket.

The thing that could prove Jesse's innocence was also the thing that would get them killed.

Once they were parked close to the truck stop, Jesse got out of the van and waited on the sidewalk for Abigail. It still felt like his brain was scrambled eggs. They walked into the truck stop together. He chose a table in the middle of the room, one that would not be completely visible from outside.

A waitress who looked like she couldn't be more than eighteen came over to them. "What can I get you folks?" Her name tag said Taylor.

"Is a waitress named Mary still around?" Abigail scooted forward in her chair.

"Mary went off shift about ten minutes ago," said Taylor.

"I'll have a coffee." Jesse glanced at the menu, choosing an item at random. "And the breakfast burrito looks good."

"I'll have the same," said Abigail.

Once the waitress left to go put in their order, Jesse's gaze rested on Abigail. "Who's Mary?"

"Just a waitress who was helpful. She called the highway patrol for me. Maybe we could do that again."

"Maybe, but we need a phone." He wasn't sure about getting the locals involved. He'd used a credit card to pay for the gas and the bed-and-breakfast. DEA would be able to track him and might have alerted the locals that he was wanted. If he was in a jail cell, it would be that much harder to prove his innocence, and Abigail would be in danger. "I think we're better off figuring this out on our own."

"Thank you for coming for me and getting me out of there. That was brave." He couldn't hide the admiration and even affection that he felt for her in that moment.

"Like I said, we're in this together, right?"

He liked the softness in her eyes when she gazed at him.

"Another agent couldn't have done better than you did, Abigail."

Color rose up in her cheeks. The rosiness made her look even prettier. "I know you would do the same for me." She stared at the table for a moment.

His heart fluttered. Jesse cleared his throat, breaking the intense moment of attraction that had formed between them.

The two men who had held him captive came into the café. They took a table that gave them a full view of where Jesse and Abigail sat.

Abigail stared at the table. "We're trapped here. What do we do now?"

The waitress set down their coffees. "Cream and sugar are right by the napkins there. Your order should be here shortly." She walked away.

Jesse waited until she was out of earshot to answer. "I'll think of something." He poured cream and sugar into his coffee.

Abigail tilted her head toward one of the big windows.

"Our van is being watched by the guy who took Dale's four-wheel drive."

They were trapped. Every move they made would be known. Nothing would happen to him or Abigail as long as they stayed where there were witnesses, but they couldn't stay here forever. He had to think of some way for them to escape.

They sat through the coffee and the meal with the two men watching them. Jesse could feel the weight of their stares as he dipped his last bite of burrito. His head had cleared enough for him to start to generate a plan. The café connected with a shop that sold things truck drivers might need.

"For starters, we're going go over to that store and get a pay-as-you-go phone," he said.

"Oh, good, I was afraid we were going to have to order more food." Abigail wiped her mouth and tossed her napkin on the table.

They stood up. He could feel the gaze of the two men on his back as he went to the counter to pay his bill. They entered the shop and walked toward the sign that indicated where the phones were. When he looked over his shoulder, the dark-haired man had left the table and was moving toward the shop.

They selected a phone and walked up to the counter. The thug meandered through the shop, positioning himself so he could keep an eye on them.

Jesse stared through the window at all the semi-trucks, some parked, some fueling up and some getting ready to pull out. They had to do something unexpected.

He squeezed Abigail's elbow as she turned away from the counter where they had paid the clerk. Outside, across the lot, a trucker crawled into the cab of his truck, clearly getting ready to pull out.

He leaned close to her ear and whispered, "Run for it."

He took the lead, sprinting toward the door that led outside. The truck's wheels had already started to rotate.

The thug from the shop raced after them. He grabbed the hem of Abigail's jacket. Before Jesse could react, Abigail whirled around, kicking the man in the shin hard enough to make him let go.

Though moving at a snail's pace, the truck was rolling through the parking lot. Abigail leaped up on the running board and swung the door open. "Can I have a ride?"

The truck driver gave a one-word answer Jesse couldn't decipher.

She crawled in. Jesse raced alongside the truck, jumped up on the running board and climbed in.

"My friend is coming with us," she said. "Hope you don't mind."

The truck driver, an older man with white hair and a bushy white beard, looked stunned but kept driving. "What are you two kids up to?" Suspicion colored his words. "Are you running from something? I got a side-arm right down here if you think you're going to try anything."

Jesse stared out the window. Larry, in Dale's four-wheel drive, had pulled up to get the dark-haired man, who had followed them out of the shop.

"We're not kids. We're with the DEA and we're on a case." He included Abigail because it had begun to feel like they were partners in this whole thing, even though she wasn't really an agent.

The truck driver pulled out onto the road, gaining speed. "Can I see your credentials?"

"I'm undercover. I don't have them with me." Jesse realized how phony his story must sound. If the guy stopped and made them get out, they'd be picked up by the thugs.

"Please believe us. We're not out to harm you in any way," Abigail said.

The truck driver gave them a nervous glance and then stared straight ahead at the road for a long moment before he spoke up. "Well, ain't that a fine kettle of fish. No doubt, you're working on slowing the drug traffic in and out of the Bakken. That place is a hole. I deliver up there. That's where I'm headed right now."

Jesse checked the side-view mirror. The two cars were following behind them.

"I don't suppose you're stopping anywhere along the way." Jesse stared at the phone, which was still in its packaging. If he could get in touch with Dale, he might be able to come and help them.

The truck driver shifted gears. "I usually pull over for a few minutes to stretch my legs. Got a schedule to keep, you know. My name is Tony, by the way."

The man seemed to be warming up to them. "I'm Jesse and this is Abigail."

"So you two are with the law?"

"I am," said Jesse.

Tony's forehead crinkled. "She's with you because...?"

"It's a long story." Jesse glanced over at Abigail. "She's been a tremendous help to me." Jesse reached over and patted Abigail's leg. "She's a very capable woman."

She offered him a warm smile, which sent a charge of electricity through him. She really was quite wonderful.

While Abigail and Tony made small talk about things they had in common, Jesse took the pay-as-you-go phone out of the packaging and activated it. He stared at it. "No signal."

They passed a sign that indicated a rest stop was twenty miles up the road.

"I'll be pulling over there just for a few minutes," said Tony.

A vague plan had started to form in Jesse's mind. He was certain the men would follow the semitruck into the rest stop. He prayed there were enough people parked at the rest stop so the men would not be able to abduct them as long as they stayed out in the open. But what then? Could they try to get to one of the vehicles and escape that way, or should they stay with the truck driver? Tony seemed like a decent man. He sure didn't want to put him in any danger.

Tony slowed his rig and hit his blinker, veering toward the exit ramp that led to the rest stop.

Jesse took in a deep breath and prayed for a clear escape route.

THIRTEEN

Abigail wondered what Jesse was thinking as Tony brought his big truck to a stop. Jesse had been staring at the phone for several minutes.

"I'm only here for five minutes," said Tony. "Long enough to use the little boys' room and stretch my legs."

"I think we won't need to ride with you any farther," said Jesse. "Your help has been much appreciated."

Tony pushed open the door. "All right, then. I wish you all the best in the world in catching the bad guys." Tony hopped down.

Abigail gripped Jesse's arm. "What are we going to do?"

Jesse opened the door.

Abigail tensed as Larry in Dale's four-wheel drive pulled into the huge parking lot. A man was also in the passenger seat.

"I'm not sure yet." He glanced around. "There are people around here. We're safe as long as we stay out in the open." He lifted the phone. "Looks like I can get a signal here. I need to get in touch with Dale."

The rest stop wasn't exactly teeming with activity. There was a motor home parked in a far corner. An older woman walked a tiny dog on a leash around the motor home. Another semitruck was pulled over at the edge of the parking area. No sign of the driver. He must be sleeping. The only other car contained a family with three kids, two running around, a boy and a girl not more than seven or eight years old. Another older child sat in the back seat of the car, his head bent as if he was reading something. Two people who must be the parents sat on a bench, looking at their phones.

The rest stop was not visible from the road due to a line of tall evergreens.

Before they had even gotten down from the truck, the car that contained one of the two men who had held Jesse captive pulled into the parking area on the opposite end of the lot from the four-wheel drive. The men had positioned their cars so that they were on either side of Tony's semitruck.

The dark-haired man got out of the four-wheel drive and paced the sidewalk by the bathrooms.

Once again, their every move would be watched. Would this be a test of wills to see who blinked first?

With Jesse walking beside her, the two of them headed toward the sidewalk, keeping their distance from the thugs. Jesse slipped his hand into Abigail's and led her toward the now-empty bench. The mom and dad had put their phones away and gotten up, and were calling to the two children running around to get back to the car. Tony came out of the bathroom, waved at them and then got up into his rig. He pulled back out onto the road.

Jesse started to dial Dale's number. He glanced at the thug on the sidewalk. "I don't know how long it is safe to stay here." He held the phone to his ear while it rang on the other end.

"What if we tried to get the car that only has one guy in it and make a run for it?"

Jesse shook his head. "Those other guys would be on us so quick."

"Even with these people around."

"I don't know. It might work." Jesse drew his attention back to the phone. "Hey, Dale."

Though she could only hear one side of the conversation, Abigail gathered the gist of the exchange. Dale had been doing lots of research and making calls. The thug Dale had overtaken at the cabin wasn't talking, though he had a record a mile long. Agent Frisk was working operations in the Bakken and had been doing so on and off for over two years. Jesse's name had been so sullied that it would be hard to find an agent high up in the chain of command who didn't think he was guilty. Jesse described the truck stop where they were.

He clicked off the phone. "He's going to get here as fast as he can."

The old lady who had been walking her dog disappeared inside the motor home. The mom and dad had gathered up their wandering children, gotten into their car and were backing out, headed toward the road.

A tense hush seemed to fall over the entire parking lot. She watched the taillights of the car that contained the family disappear behind the trees that blocked the view of the road.

Larry, the thug in the four-wheel drive, got out of the car and edged toward them. The third man got out of his car, as well.

Abigail glanced at the semitruck and then the motor

home, which had its curtains drawn. She prayed that another car would pull into the rest stop or that the people in the motor home would come back out.

Jesse whispered, barely moving his mouth. "Back away. We can't run toward the road. They'll cut us off."

"Maybe we can get to the motor home," she said. She didn't like the idea of putting the old woman in any danger.

Together they both burst to their feet just as the men made a run for them. Their path to the motor home was cut-off.

"Let's try to circle back around," said Jesse.

They hurried to the back of the rest stop, which had a small pond with ducks swimming in it. Jesse ran toward the trees that surrounded the water.

Abigail glanced over her shoulder. The men emerged from either side of the building. They wouldn't be able to get back to the parking.

They ran for ten minutes. The men stayed close at their heels.

A single gunshot reverberated behind them. They ran out into an open field. Two of the men, Larry and the dark-haired man, chased after them. The soil in the field had been turned over for planting. Their shoes sank down in the soft dirt. Jesse raced toward a corner of the field, where a piece of farm equipment stood.

One of the men fired off another shot. The bullet came so close to hitting her that her eardrum felt like it had been hit with a tiny mallet. Reflexively, she drew her hand up to her ear.

Jesse sprinted toward the enclosed tractor that sat in the corner of the field. He jumped up and swung the door open. "Get in."

The men were about forty yards away.

Abigail climbed into the cab of the tractor with Jesse right behind her. He gripped the steering wheel and stared at the control panel, and then at what was probably a gearshift. "How do you operate this thing? We'll just take it to the edge of the field, so the farmer can still find it. It'll provide cover and give us a head start."

The men were getting closer. One of them had stopped to raise his gun again.

Abigail looked at the dials on the tractor and saw a key. She turned it and the tractor roared to life. "Looks like you have a clutch and a brake down there."

A bullet pinged off the metal of the tractor cab as it jerked into motion.

Abigail slipped lower in the seat. Through the back window of the tractor, she could see the men still running toward them.

Jesse increased the speed of the tractor. "This isn't exactly NASCAR."

They were maybe going fifteen miles an hour. Though the men continued to run after them, they slowed as the distance between them increased.

She lifted her head and craned her neck. The landscape was completely flat. The men were still making their way across the field, though they had become small figures in the distance.

The tractor bumped along. There wasn't really any road around here.

"Take my phone and let Dale know what's happened." Jesse recited the number for Abigail. "The other guy must have waited back at the rest stop. I don't want Dale to run into an ambush."

Dale picked up on the first ring. "I'm on my way."

Abigail told him the situation, explaining they had run at least a mile behind the rest stop, with no roads or landmarks in sight.

Dale paused for a moment. "I can't find you unless you can get up to a road or some landmark that would show up on GPS."

She stared out at the barren land. There was not so much as a farmhouse in sight, let alone a road they could identify. "We'll let you know as soon as we're in a place where you can come to us."

"Let me look at a map on my phone and see if I can tell you where the closest road would be in relation to the rest stop and the direction you ran," said Dale. "I'll call you back."

"Okay." She clicked off. Their phone was a cheap model that wouldn't pull up any maps. Would an area as remote as this even be mapped?

They came to the edge of the field.

The tractor motor made a grinding noise as the flat land turned into rolling hills with tall, thick, wild grass.

"We better get out," Jesse said. "The farmer needs to be able to find his tractor when he comes looking for it."

They climbed out of the cab. In all directions, they saw rolling hills. She saw no fences. No power lines. The tractor was the last sign that they were anywhere near people. The farms and ranches in this part of the world might be thousands of acres.

Jesse clamped a hand on Abigail's shoulder. "You're the one who knows how to navigate in the wilderness."

Maybe so, but she was used to reading mountainous terrain. She looked around, trying to get her bearings. From the rest stop, they had run west. "I say we head in the general direction of where that main highway is that leads into the Bakken, but do a wide circle around where that field was so we don't risk running into those men."

"Lead the way."

Minutes after they started walking, raindrops pelted her skin. In the distance, she saw what looked like a cabin or a barn, weathered gray by time and leaning to one side. They ran across the grassy field toward the shelter of a building that had probably not been inhabited for a hundred years.

As they drew closer to the building, she saw that it had once been a homestead. What might have been a wooden trough was off to one side, and there was a pile of logs and gray boards behind the house, which was maybe some sort of outbuilding. The drizzle of rain turned into a downpour as they slipped inside.

Though it was overcast, some light shone through the holes in the roof, and rain dripped from the rafters. She chose a corner of the room that didn't seem to be leaking.

Jesse remained standing, staring at his cell phone. "I can't get a signal."

Abigail slipped down the wall to the floorboards that seemed relatively stable. Though it didn't surprise her, not having a cell phone signal made her feel even more hopeless. Dale couldn't reach them to say what he had found on his maps.

She peered out the opening where there used to be a door. Though the rain reduced visibility, she couldn't see the men anywhere. Chances were, they would have sought shelter from the rain, as well. Maybe they would even hike back to the rest stop, but she knew better than to count on that.

Feeling a sense of despair, Abigail took in a breath and closed her eyes. "So what do we do now?"

Abigail sounded weary. He didn't blame her. He was battling a loss of hope himself. They might as well be stuck back up on that mountain, for all the good the cell phone did them. He sat down beside her, close enough that their shoulders were touching.

He closed his eyes and listened to the soothing sound of the rain.

Her hand rested on top of his. "Maybe the first thing we should do is pray."

Her hand was smooth as silk against his rough fingers. "Yes, I'd like that." Seeing her faith in the face of such adversity had restored some of his.

She closed her eyes and prayed, asking God for guidance. A tender silence fell between them, with only the whispering whooshing of the rain coming down.

She squeezed his hand. "Amen. I'm glad you decided to pray with me."

He opened his eyes and turned toward her. Her lips curled up in a faint smile. She leaned toward him. Though the sky was grey and cloud covered, there seemed to be light coming from her. He recognized the glow of affection in her features. His chest felt like it was being squeezed in a vise. Could he open his heart to her? After Melissa's death, he had felt as though his heart had turned to stone. Never again did he want to experience the helplessness of loving someone and not being able to save them.

"Thank you for all you've done for me, Abigail. You're amazing."

She pulled her knees up toward her chest. "Not too bad for a small-town girl, huh?"

He loved sitting beside her. Even in such trying circumstances, being with her nourished him. "Not too bad at all."

She kicked at the floorboards. "What if we hid the hard drive here? They would never think to come look here. We could come back for it when you're ready to make your case."

"I like the way you think, but could we even find this place again? I was hoping we could pass it to Dale for safekeeping." He stared at his phone again.

"Then we should head out. Those men are either slowed or stopped by the rain," she said. "We'll get to a spot where we can get a signal sooner or later."

He listened to the downpour outside and the dribbling off the roof. "Abigail, you've got a lot of spunk and nerves of steel."

"It would give us the head start we need. Besides, what's a little rain?" she said. "I've guided people to safety in freak snowstorms."

He gazed at her and nodded. "Okay." He jumped to his feet and held a hand out for her. Her fingers clasped his and he pulled her to her feet. They stood for a moment facing each other, their noses nearly touching. The electric charge of attraction pulsed all around him, enveloping him like a warm blanket.

"We should get moving," she said. Her turning away seemed to cut off the intensity of the moment.

They rushed out into the downpour. Because the terrain was so flat, he could see the rain coming from the sky in solid gray sheets for miles. There were pockets where no rain was falling.

Abigail walked with a determined step. "We should head due south. That way we'll be moving parallel to that field. When we think we've gotten past it, we can turn east, which should put us out on the road."

"I'm glad you're the navigator," he said.

As they walked side by side, he found himself sneaking glances at her. Then his hand slipped into hers. She held on tight as if to confirm that she had the same feelings.

Through the murkiness of the downpour, he could see another figure moving toward them. A man alone in dark clothes. It could be a farmer, or it could be one of the thugs still searching for them.

As they walked, the faraway figure turned and headed in their direction, closing the distance between them. Though they were at least a mile apart, it was clear now that he was headed toward them, and it probably wasn't a farmer coming for a friendly chat. The blurred figure changed his stalking pace into a jog.

Though there were clusters of trees, there was really no place to conceal themselves. They quickened their pace, their feet squishing in the mud when they came to a different field, where the soil had also been plowed for planting. The man edged steadily toward them until he was close enough they could see it was the dark-haired man.

As his clothes got wetter, a chill permeated Jesse's skin and settled into his bones. Abigail still had her waterproof jacket, though her pants looked soaked. They hurried across the flat terrain. He had to let go of her hand so they could run faster.

"I think we can go ahead and make a turn toward where the road should be." She was out of breath as she spoke, glancing over her shoulder at their pursuer. "There's no way to shake him, is there?"

Jesse kept jogging as he talked. "We've just got to keep moving faster than he does."

The figure was still coming toward them, showing an impressive amount of stamina. If they could just stay far enough ahead so the man couldn't get a shot with a pistol, they might be able to make it to the road alive and call Dale.

His muscles felt fatigued as they jogged across an open area with tall, lumpy grass weighed down by wind and rain. Abigail slowed, as well.

She stopped, bending over to rest her hands above her knees. "I just need to catch my breath."

The thug kept coming toward them, never slowing down, never tiring. Jesse tugged on her sleeve. "Abigail, we've got to keep moving."

She took in a ragged breath and nodded. Their run had slowed to a jog, though they kept moving despite being soaked to the bone, despite the fatigue that was overtaking both of them.

Jesse willed himself to keep moving. Across the wide, flat plain, he saw the road up ahead. The gray of the paving was so distorted by the rain that it almost looked like a mirage.

Seeing the road gave him the incentive to keep moving. Maybe a car would go by and they could catch a ride. When he glanced over his shoulder, the thug had stopped. He was close enough that Jesse could make out that he had pulled out his phone and was making a call.

Jesse's brief moment of thinking they could make it to safety was shattered.

Now that the thug had a clear location on them that he could communicate to the others, it meant even more men would be coming after them.

FOURTEEN

Abigail's lungs were sore from breathing so intensely. As she forced herself to keep moving, her leg muscles felt leaden. Her clothes must weigh an extra five pounds from all the water they'd absorbed. The road was closer, but getting to it had been a sort of false hope. The thug was only jogging toward them. Now that he'd made his phone call and had ushered even more manpower down on them, he didn't have to catch them, only keep an eye on them, which was easy enough to do when the flat land stretched for miles.

She recalled how the dark-haired man had brought the dogs into the mountains via helicopter to track them. Clearly, whoever was behind this, probably the Agent Frisk the dead man had mentioned in the video, had all kinds of resources beyond just the three men who had chased them from the rest stop.

Jesse stopped and pulled out his phone. "If he had a signal, then we have one, too." He pressed the keypad as he walked. "Keep running, Abigail. I'll catch up."

She jogged ahead. The road was within twenty yards, though there was no sign of a car coming in either direction. Maybe that was a good thing. It meant the thugs weren't close by—but it also meant there was no one who might give them temporary refuge in the form of a ride.

As her feet pounded the ground, she glanced over her shoulder. The dark-haired man was looming dangerously close to Jesse as he jogged and talked on the phone. Would Dale even be able to get to them in time?

She ran faster. A gunshot sounded behind her. All the air left her lungs. She craned her neck. Jesse was lying on the ground with the thug bearing down on him, his gun raised. Time seemed to stand still. She slowed and turned. She couldn't leave Jesse. If they both died here, so be it. She picked up a rock and ran toward Jesse. It was no match for a gun, but it was all she had.

Jesse bolted up from the ground and ran toward her. Relief spread through her like a burst of sunshine on a cloudy day. He hadn't been hit. He'd avoided the bullet by dropping to the ground.

Jesse gestured that she needed to keep running. She turned back around and headed toward the road. She stumbled when another shot was fired, but when she craned her neck, she saw Jesse sprinting toward her.

The thug who had to stop to fire off the shots was some distance behind him. Jesse caught up with her just as her feet touched the pavement of the road.

"Dale has been looking for us on the road." Jesse never slowed in his run. Because he was out of breath from running, his words came slowly. "We need to find a mile marker, so he knows where we are. Keep running."

The long straight road stretched before them. Maybe a mile away, the road rounded up over a hill and dropped out of sight. Up ahead, she saw the little green metal sign that would tell them where they were. The thug remained at their heels. They'd be slowed down when Jesse made the to call Dale again. Her only prayer was that Dale could get to them before the thugs did.

The green metal sign indicated they were at mile marker fifty-seven. She was pretty sure they were headed in the direction of the rest stop, though she had no idea how far away they were from it. She hadn't paid attention to the mile markers when they'd ridden with Tony.

Jesse kept running. "That guy is too close for me to slow down to make the call to Dale."

She still held the rock she'd picked up. Not much of a weapon. Though they weren't armed, there were two of them and only one thug. Was there a way to ambush him before he had a chance to aim the gun at them? There were clusters of trees not far from the road, but the thug would be able to see them running toward them for cover.

"What if we slow down?" Her feet pounded the concrete of the road.

"What?"

"So he thinks he can hit us. Then he'll use up his bullets."

"Good idea. But I'll do it. You stay ahead of me." Jesse's run turned into a jog.

Abigail slowed but increased the distance between herself and Jesse. There was no time to argue with him over who should be the target.

How many shots had the man fired so far? Three, maybe?

The tactic was a dangerous one. What if the dark-haired man wounded Jesse?

Two more shots were fired. Each time, Abigail's

heart stopped. She kept running but looked over her shoulder. Jesse was still behind her, still moving.

She prayed that they would both get out of this alive. *Oh, God, please help us.*

Without warning, the downpour turned to hail the size of quarters. She put her arms up to shield herself from the pelting. The storm was so intense she couldn't see more than a few feet in front of her.

Jesse was by her side, grasping her elbow and leading her off the road toward the shelter of the trees. Her skin stung from the hail hitting her. He pulled her beneath the trees, which provided only partial shelter.

When she peered out, she couldn't see where the thug was because of the intensity of the downpour.

"You all right?" Jesse wrapped his arms around her shoulder and drew her close.

"I feel like I've gone ten rounds with a prizefighter." It was nice to have Jesse's protective arm around her.

The storm sounded like a million pieces of bubble wrap being broken at the same time. Visibility was so reduced, she couldn't even see the road.

"Yeah, I'm pretty beat-up, also." Jesse leaned forward, looking all around. "That guy must have run for cover, too. I don't see him anywhere."

He squeezed her shoulder. She peered up at him, looking into his deep brown eyes. The moment was only a brief reprieve, but she relished it all the same. They'd be on the run again as soon as the storm let up. Even though their situation was tenuous and escape from harm felt like a long shot, she realized there was no other place she'd rather be than here with Jesse.

She peered out again. The clusters of trees were

barely discernable through the onslaught of hail. "I wonder where he went."

Jesse stood beside her, their shoulders touching. He shook his head and pointed at a dark patch across the road through the thick sheets of hail. "That would have been the closest place for him to run."

The intensity of the hail hitting the ground changed as the downpour let up a little. Headlights glared through the haze of the storm up the road.

Jesse pulled out his phone and clicked the screen. "I'm texting the mile marker number." He clicked the screen and then brought it close to his face to read Dale's response. "Dale says he's close."

They waited while the hail continued to spill out of the sky. In the distance, the murky glow of headlights appeared on the road.

Jesse held up the phone, turning the flashlight on and off. The vehicle slowed and flashed its headlights.

"That's the signal. It's him." Jesse burst out from the shelter of the trees.

Even as the driving hail stung her skin, her spirits lifted. They ran toward the headlights as the vehicle slowed and pulled over, though Dale kept the headlights on.

A gunshot cracked the air around them. Abigail startled into alertness. The falling hail distorted noise so much, she wasn't sure where the shot had even come from.

Jesse grabbed her hand and guided her toward the soft-focus headlights of Dale's vehicle.

On the other side of the road, she saw a dark, moving blob. That had to be the dark-haired man with the gun.

In the distance, she spotted another set of headlights coming toward Dale's vehicle.

Dale's SUV was in motion once again, heading toward them even as the other car closed the distance between them.

Another shot was fired, though it seemed to fizzle as soon as it left the gun. The dark blob became more distinct.

The other set of headlights was within yards of Dale's car. The body of the blue SUV Dale drove materialized out of the storm. The car slowed to maybe five miles an hour.

Her hand reached for a door handle and she fell into the back seat. Jesse had yanked open the passenger-side door in the front.

She was soaked, and it felt like she'd been beaten with a thousand tiny sticks. All the same, the worn muddy interior of Dale's back seat brought more relief than a soft bed or a hot bath.

"Boy, are we glad to see you," said Jesse.

The car behind them hit Dale's rear bumper with intense force, sending a new wave of terror shooting through Abigail's body.

Jesse's body flung forward toward the dashboard. His chest hit something solid, and then, as if he was being lifted by the back of his coat, his back banged against the seat. He was fumbling for the seat belt when a second jolt hit the back bumper again, though this one wasn't as jarring. Dale pressed the gas and gained some speed.

Dale's windshield wipers worked furiously to clear the hail and provide some visibility. Jesse stared through the windshield. At best, he could see only a murky impression of the road. Over and over, the center yellow line popped into view for a fraction of a second.

The hail hitting the metal of the SUV made it feel like the body of the car would split into a thousand pieces. The intensity of the assault surrounded them.

Jesse craned his neck to glance at Abigail and then out the back window. The headlights of the other car were two out-of-focus circles. The other car slowed down and then stopped, probably to pick up the dark-haired man. Jesse rested his gaze on Abigail, who had a stunned expression on her face as she buckled herself in. "You all right?"

She nodded. "Just a little shook up." And then she smiled, reached forward and covered his hand with hers where it rested on the back of the seat. "But glad to be here in Dale's car with you."

The words *with you* echoed in his head as the warmth of her touch soaked through his skin.

Yeah, he thought, *I really know how to show a lady a good time.* When all this was over, maybe he could take her out for a nice dinner as a thank-you. He felt a tightening in his chest as he spotted the headlights of the other car still behind them...if all of this was ever going to be over.

"What do we do now?" Abigail leaned back in the seat.

Dale hunched over the steering wheel, his neck strained so his face was closer to the windshield. "First, we lose these guys."

With the reduced visibility, the SUV topped out at sixty. Even that was a scary speed to be traveling. The noise of the tires rolling over payment broke up.

"Whoa, we're on the shoulder." Dale jerked the steering wheel. "Sorry about that."

The other car gained on them. The headlights looked to be about ten feet behind them.

Dale sped up. Without warning, a tree filled the whole of the windshield. They'd gone off the road. Dale swerved again. This time the vehicle fishtailed.

Every muscle in Jesse's body tensed as he gripped the dashboard.

Dale slowed down.

Though Jesse could not be sure, it appeared that the road curved off at a slight angle. The headlights of the other vehicle filled the cab of theirs.

Abigail's frightened voice pierced his awareness. "They're right behind us."

Dale pressed the gas. Tension tainted with terror filled his words. "Not to worry. We've been in tough situations like this before, right?"

Jesse swallowed. His mouth had gone completely dry. "Sure, nothing we can't handle." Dale was a cool cucumber. For him to show any sign of fear was not good.

The other car collided with their bumper, jarring Jesse in his seat. His heart pounded wildly.

Dale pressed the gas.

They were trapped. If they went too fast, they risked losing control of the SUV. If they slowed to a safe speed, the other car would be able to run them off the road.

He felt another bump, this time on the side of Dale's vehicle toward the back. Their back end swung out. Dale gripped the steering wheel; his knuckles were white, his eyes drawn into narrow slits and the veins popping up in his neck.

"There's a gun in the glove compartment," said Dale. "Maybe you can try to take it out."

Jesse reached toward the glove compartment.

"I think I could get a better shot at them from the back seat." Abigail's words seemed to come from a far-away place. "Hand it to me."

Jesse felt himself leaning forward toward the glove compartment while the rush of the storm and the incessant tapping of the hail on the car surrounded him. He opened the glove box and reached for the gun.

Everything after that happened in slow motion. Jesse felt like he was experiencing it while numb or underwater. As Dale's SUV caught air and turned at an odd angle, he wasn't sure if it was because they had been hit again or because Dale had gone off the road.

The SUV landed and bumped along, then twisted. They were floating through the air again. The vehicle was halfway upside down. Abigail screamed. And then the hood of the vehicle scraped across rough terrain for what felt like miles before they came to a stop.

Metal continued to shake and vibrate. Jesse opened his mouth to say something but no words came out. He was upside down, his head pressing against the roof of the SUV, the seat belt cutting into his chest and stomach.

He looked over at Dale. His eyes were closed. His face had gone white as rice and a trickle of blood ran past his temple.

Jesse was coherent enough to know that shock was setting in. He had to fight it. He reached toward Dale and shook his shoulder. Dale was unresponsive.

It was a challenge to get out even a single word, but he managed to utter Abigail's name. The cacophony of the hail beating against the SUV and the rush of the storm around him seemed to be turned up to an even higher volume. Abigail did not answer.

His heart squeezed tight. He struggled to take in a breath. Once again, he had the sensation of drowning, drifting deeper and deeper underwater. He was coherent enough to realize his body was going into shock.

Not today. He wasn't going to lose Abigail today or any day.

He fought to shake himself free of the numbness that threatened to envelop him.

Then he heard Abigail's sweet, soft voice. She uttered a word he couldn't quite make out. But she was alive. His mind cleared as though he had broken through the surface of the water and was gasping for air.

He wasn't sure if he said, "I'm going to get you out," or if he just thought it. But he found himself reaching to unbuckle his seat belt. He rolled around. His shoulders and back rested against the roof of the vehicle. Dale still hadn't moved.

If he thought about losing his friend, the numbness of shock would take over again.

I'll get you out, too.

He turned and reached for the door handle. He had to push all his weight against it as it scraped the ground. There was enough of an opening for him to crawl out on his belly. He pulled himself through with his hands, clawing the muddy ground. Hail stabbed at his skin.

Without getting to his feet, he dragged himself to the back of the SUV, where Abigail was. The hood was bent and compressed. He wouldn't be able to get the door open. The window glass was still in place but broken.

He poked his head back into the open front door.

"Abigail, I can't get the door open. I'm going to have to break the window and pull you through that way."

Only the sound of the storm answered back. He wondered how extensive her injuries were.

He pressed his lips together and then took in a breath. "Can you hear me?"

"Yes" was the faint reply. "I think I can scoot toward the other side of the car while you break the window."

Relief spread through him. "Good."

By sitting on his behind, he was able to kick the glass out of the back window. He found a rock, broke the remainder of the glass out and then tried to brush most of the shards out of the way with the same rock. He poked his head in.

She looked like a scared animal crouching in a dark corner.

"Be careful coming through. There's still some sharp pieces in the frame and glass on the ground." He scraped some more of the glass out of the way with the rock. "Okay, crawl on through."

The hail, which had turned to rain again, slashed against his cheek and trickled down the back of his neck. He didn't hear any movement inside the cab of the SUV. He poked his head in and reached his hand toward Abigail, who had gotten down on all fours, prepared to crawl toward the window. He could barely make out her features in the darkness of the crushed vehicle.

"Sorry, I'm…just a little shook up." Her voice faltered.

"Understandable." He didn't want to rush her, but he was pretty sure the thugs in the car that had run them off the road were searching for them. He reached a hand out toward her. "I got you." He half pulled, half guided her through the narrow opening.

Once she was out, he helped her to her feet. All around him all he could see was rain and the impression of objects like trees, rocks and grass. Everything was out of focus but stationary. No moving objects were coming toward them.

The crash had so disoriented him he wasn't even sure which way the road was. "Let's go get Dale out." He navigated around to the driver's side of the SUV.

Abigail pressed close behind him.

He dreaded dragging Dale out and discovering he was not alive. But when he got to the driver's side, the door had been pushed open. He peered inside. Dale was not there anymore. The back of the seat was high enough to shield the view of the front seat. The door had been opened so quietly that he hadn't heard it above the storm and his focus on Abigail. His first thought was that the thugs had gotten to Dale.

Abigail gripped his arm.

Before they had time to react, a man with a gun emerged from the gray sheets of the storm. Jesse recognized him as the man referred to as an associate, the man who had tortured him.

The man pointed the gun at them and lifted his chin. "I think you folks better come with me."

FIFTEEN

Abigail stared down the barrel of the gun as her pulse drummed in her ears. Without thinking about it, she reached for Jesse's hand. She could see the wheels turning inside his head. He was trying to come up with a plan of escape.

The man with the gun turned slightly and pointed. "About-face and start marching that way."

Though she could not see more than a few feet in front of her, Abigail pivoted and took several steps. A plan formed in her mind. She squeezed Jesse's hand, hoping he would understand.

She stumbled. "My leg hurts." And then she fell, hoping it looked believable.

Panic filled the voice of the man with the gun. "Get up, now!"

While the associate was focused on Abigail, Jesse jumped him, reaching for the gun. The two men wrestled, falling to the muddy ground. The man still held on to the gun. Jesse maneuvered himself to be on top of him, where he landed a blow across the man's face. The man fired a shot, but it went off to the side, low to the ground.

Abigail reached for the gun, trying to yank it out of the man's hand while Jesse restrained him. She grabbed the gun and turned it on the man.

An arm wrapped around Abigail's neck, so her chin jammed into the second thug's elbow. Then she felt the cold barrel of a gun against her temple.

The voice behind her was sinister. "I think you better drop that gun right now, little lady."

Jesse got off the man he'd wrestled to the ground and held up his hands. "Do what he says, Abigail." He glanced off to the side before resting his gaze on her.

She wondered if there was a third man behind the one who held her in a neck lock.

Abigail let the gun fall to the ground, and the man who had found them grabbed it and scrambled to his feet.

The thug who held the gun to her head spoke to the other man. "You know what to do with him."

The associate pointed the gun at Jesse. "Start walking."

Abigail watched as the rain swallowed up both men. She felt an intense panic at being separated from him. "Where are you taking him?"

The man who held the gun to her head pressed his mouth close to her ear. "Somewhere you two can't get any bright ideas together. Now, turn around and start walking."

When she turned around, she saw that a third man had been standing behind them—the dark-haired man who had been after them since they'd run through the mountains.

The dark-haired man crossed his arms. "Well, look what we have here."

The other man, who she remembered was Larry, let go of her but poked the gun in the middle of her back.

They walked for a hundred feet or so. Because of the downpour, she didn't so much see the road as it materialized beneath her feet. They led her toward Dale's four-wheel drive.

Larry searched her. His hand touched the hard drive in her pocket. Before they even pulled it out, she felt an overwhelming sense of defeat.

Defeat sank in around her. This was it. They would probably shoot her now.

Larry handed the hard drive over to the dark-haired man, who pulled out his phone, turned away and started talking in a hushed tone. She couldn't hear the conversation, but she thought she heard mention of Jesse's name. She feared that the order had been given to shoot both her and Jesse. What bothered her most of all was that she and Jesse would not die together. They would have no parting words, no chance even for a kiss. She would never get the chance to tell Jesse how much she cared about him.

The dark-haired man turned back to stare at Abigail. He seemed to end his conversation when he said, "Okay, you're the boss." Once he clicked off the phone, he reached up with his gun and hit Abigail in the side of the head with it.

She swayed and then collapsed...

She regained consciousness long enough to realize she was lying on the back seat of a car. As her awareness faded, her last thought was of Jesse. What had become of him? Was he alive? She wasn't sure why, now that they had the hard drive, she hadn't been shot outright. Maybe they were taking her some place her body wouldn't be found.

What had happened to Dale? Had they gotten to him, too?

The car rumbled down the road as the blackness surrounded her again.

When she came to, she found herself in a room that looked like it had been the pantry of an industrial kitchen at one time. There were no windows. The shelves still had spilled flour on them. A few bulk-size cans with faded, dirty and torn labels remained on the shelves, and rice was scattered across the floor.

She rose unsteadily on her feet. She had no memory of how she'd gotten here. She walked toward the door and shook the handle. Of course, it was locked. Though the room was probably ten feet square, the walls felt like they were closing in on her. Her breathing became shallow. She was trapped in here.

She moved toward the shelves that contained the bulk cans. One was for stewed tomatoes; the other looked like it was some kind of beans. She didn't see a can opener anywhere, only a piece of twisted metal that maybe had been part of an industrial mixer at one time.

She stood for a long moment, listening. Outside the walls of this room, she heard an odd whirring noise. The rhythm remained the same, like a huge fan.

Was she being left here to die, to starve to death? That way the men who had been after her and Jesse for so long wouldn't risk being tracked down for murder.

Abigail slumped down on the floor as a sense of despair seeped into her bones and muscles. Had she and Jesse come this far only to have it end this way?

She refused to let herself cry. She was a strong and capable woman—qualities that Brent had resented but that Jesse seemed to celebrate. Her heart fluttered when she thought of Jesse. But the sparkle faded quickly. She deeply regretted not telling him how she felt about him. And now, it appeared that it was too late.

She tilted her head and let out a prayer-filled breath. What was she even praying for? That God would show her a way out of this room? That she would get a chance to tell Jesse that she loved him? She couldn't even put words to the desperation she felt.

She opened her eyes after her wordless prayer. Something near the ceiling caught her eye. She stepped toward the corner of the room, where a camera was mounted. The installment of the camera must have been recent; it was the only thing in the room not covered in dust.

She was being watched. Oddly, the presence of the camera renewed her hope. They were keeping her alive for some reason.

The rope that bound Jesse's hands cut into his wrists. He'd been sitting on the hard, wooden chair for at least a half hour with no one coming to check on him. He'd been brought here with a hood over his head, after being hauled in the back of a car for at least two hours. Right before he'd been put in this room, they'd torn the hood off his head.

Two questions raged through his mind. What had become of Abigail, and why were they keeping him alive? They must have found the hard drive in her jacket pocket. He refused to consider that she might be dead.

Shot and dragged into the brush on some rural stretch of road. He could not give in to that kind of despair.

He also wondered what had happened to Dale. Had his friend crawled away and died, been killed or escaped?

He wiggled in the chair. His bottom was sore from sitting. He rose to his feet and walked around. The room looked like it had been some sort of control room for watching something. There were banks of instruments, along with several monitors.

There were two doors on opposite walls. When he checked, both of them were locked.

The room had a line of small windows that allowed light in, but they were too high up for him to see out of. With his foot, he scooted the chair toward the windows. Though his balance was off because his hands were tied behind his back, he managed to stand on the chair and then raise himself on tiptoe.

He saw a series of metal buildings, maybe barracks of some sort. In the distance, a single drilling rig still turned. Several others were inert. He must be in the Bakken. This place now looked abandoned but had probably been a boomtown at the height of the oil activity. He saw several cars, one of them Dale's four-wheel drive the thugs had taken. He caught a flash of a man walking around the buildings holding a rifle, and another man was sitting on top of a car hood holding a handgun. The place was being guarded, but the men didn't seem to be on high alert.

A key turned in a lock and the door swung open. He nearly fell off the chair when he turned to see who it was.

"Ah, Agent Santorum. I see you have made yourself at home."

The man standing before him was Agent Frisk. Frisk, a man in his forties, had wavy hair that reached his shoulders and a five o'clock shadow. He wore workman's clothes, coveralls and a flannel shirt. The impression Jesse had of his appearance was that Agent Frisk was playing a part. When he wasn't undercover, Frisk was clean-shaven and his hair was cropped close to his head. Jesse didn't know that much about Agent Frisk. He'd only worked a couple of operations with him, the last being the one in Mexico where Lee Bronson had died. Agent Frisk had always seemed efficient but aloof.

Jesse stepped off the chair.

Agent Frisk closed the door behind him. The keys were on a ring, which he placed on one of the dusty counters. The handle of a gun stuck out from one of his coverall pockets. Agent Frisk gestured theatrically. "Please, have a seat."

Jesse remained standing. Even though his hands were tied, he needed to look for an opportunity to overtake Agent Frisk, but he couldn't do that sitting down.

Agent Frisk squared his shoulders. Though his voice remained level, his eyes narrowed and his jawline turned to granite. "I said have a seat, Agent Santorum." His hand fluttered over his gun.

"You're not going to use that. You kept me alive for some reason."

"You always were a smart man." Agent Frisk let his hand fall to his side. "I assure you that could be a very temporary situation."

Jesse still didn't sit down.

Agent Frisk paced. "I suppose you want to know why

I didn't have you killed once we got the hard drive off your partner."

Jesse felt as though he'd been punched in the stomach twice. They had the hard drive. All of this had been for nothing, and now it might have cost him Abigail. Sweet, funny Abigail. "What have you done with her?"

Agent Frisk made a tsk-tsking noise and held out his palm toward Jesse. "All in good time." He turned to face Jesse. "I really think you're going to want to be sitting down for this."

The words held an intense coldness to them. Jesse sat down, partly because his knees were weak over the news he feared he was about to get concerning Abigail, and partly because he thought it might make Agent Frisk be less guarded. Maybe if Frisk didn't think he was going to be overtaken at any second, Jesse could wait for an opportunity to escape.

Frisk paced, stretching the moment out, increasing the tension in the room.

Jesse felt as though he was pulling up each word from the ends of his toes. "What. Have. You. Done. With. Abigail?"

"Patience. This story takes a while to tell."

Jesse clenched his jaw, enraged at the way Frisk was toying with him, taking sick pleasure at Jesse's anguish.

Frisk stopped pacing. He leaned against the counter. "What was on that hard drive could have put me away and probably exonerated you."

"I take it you destroyed the hard drive."

Frisk lifted his chin. The look of triumph on his face told Jesse everything he needed to know. "Lee Bronson was a good little soldier...up until the end, when he grew a conscience."

"He wanted out. He was just trying to pay the medical bills for his kid." Jesse shook his head.

"It was pure coincidence that you were at the operation the night he died."

"You shot him," said Jesse.

"Who's to say?" Frisk glanced at his fingernails and then grinned. "Gunfire was coming from everywhere."

A chill seeped into Jesse's skin and traveled to his bones. He shivered. He knew he was looking into the face of pure evil. Frisk was a man so consumed with the need for power and wealth, he would stop at nothing to get it and keep it.

Frisk folded his arms over his chest. "Anyway, Lee did a good job of making it look like you were the tainted DEA agent. So it got me to thinking. Things are drying up here in the Bakken. Less oil being pumped, fewer customers." Frisk turned and looked directly at Jesse. His light blue eyes were unsettling. "I want out, and I want out clean. The groundwork is already laid for you being dirty. Why not have you confess to running product in the Bakken?"

Jesse couldn't get a deep breath. His lungs felt like they were in a vise, being twisted tighter and tighter. "I never ran an operation in the Bakken."

Frisk pushed himself off the counter and took several steps toward Jesse. "You don't have to have lived here to have set up the supply line for the drugs."

"I would never confess to such a thing," Jesse said.

Frisk leaned over so his nose was almost touching Jesse's. "Oh, I think you will." He straightened up and walked back toward the counter where the dusty monitors were. "This is quite a neat setup here. When they were pumping tons of oil out of the ground, they needed a way to monitor the equipment and the workers."

He leaned forward and clicked on one of the monitors. Frisk's body blocked Jesse's view of the screen. "It just took a little rewiring and setting up a camera for what I'm about to show you." He stepped to one side so Jesse had a view of the monitor.

Jesse's heart seized up when he saw Abigail crouched on the floor in a windowless room.

Frisk pulled a phone out of his shirt pocket. "I need you to enter the room where target two is being held." There was a moment of silence before Frisk responded. "Yes, you know the plan."

Jesse watched in horror as the door where Abigail was being kept swung open and a man with a gun entered, grabbed Abigail by the back of her collar and yanked her to her feet. The thug turned her so she was looking directly at the camera and placed the gun on her temple.

Frisk reached over and turned off the monitor.

"So you see, Agent Santorum, you will confess, and I will tape your confession and send it on over to DEA."

Frisk walked over to an object covered in a tarp. He tore off the cover, revealing a camera. "I think we're all ready to begin filming."

Jesse's stomach tightened into a hard knot as he struggled to keep a clear head. The thought of losing Abigail tore him to pieces.

SIXTEEN

With the gun pointed at her head, all Abigail could think about was getting away. Why, now, did they want to make sure she was seen on camera with her life being threatened? Who was watching on the other side?

The thug pulled the gun away from her head.

"You're not going to kill me?" Her heart was still pounding wildly as she turned to face the man who had held a gun to her head. The thug was someone she had not seen before. A young man with red hair. He was maybe twenty years old, a kid, really. She took a step toward him.

He held the gun up. "Back off."

"I'm sorry, I just want to know why they're keeping me here. What was that little theater game all about? I thought you were going to kill me."

"I'm just following orders." The man's hand was trembling as he held the gun on her.

He was afraid. She might be able to overtake him, but there was a huge risk that doing that would send ten men down on her if she was being watched on camera.

Her voice filled with compassion. "I'm sure you're just following orders."

The man edged toward the door, still pointing the gun at her. The door behind him was probably still unlocked.

She glanced up at the camera, where a red light glowed above the lens. This might be her only possibility for escape. She whirled around, grabbed the man at the wrist and drove the hand that held the gun upward. The martial arts lessons she'd been dragged to by her brothers kicked in.

The man was stronger than she had expected. He held on to the gun. She punched him in the stomach. When he doubled over, she clasped her hands together and hit his back. He groaned in pain. The gun flew across the floor.

The man straightened, his face red with anger. She had miscalculated because of the man's age. He was just as violent as the others.

She turned and lunged toward where the gun had slid across the floor. The man grabbed her jacket and yanked her backward. He swung her around with such force, she fell to the floor. Again, she crawled toward the gun. Her fingers were within inches of clasping the handle when she was dragged back across the floor on her stomach.

The man was out of breath. "You make this way too hard, lady." His cowboy boots pounded the concrete floor. He reached down and picked up the gun.

There was no one between her and the door. She scrambled to her feet and reached for the handle. She pushed down on it and the door opened. Light flooded in from the windows in the other room, which was some sort of cafeteria, now dusty and abandoned.

The man pulled her back by grabbing her hair. He

got between her and the door, pointed the gun at her and pressed the door shut with his back. He looked ruffled and upset. His cheeks were crimson, and his freckles were even more prominent. "Get back." He waved the gun. "Step back toward that corner and keep your hands up where I can see them."

She gulped in air, put up her hands and stepped toward a far corner of the room.

The man reached behind him for the door handle, still watching her. "I gotta hand it to you, lady. You put up a good fight."

He disappeared behind the door. Even as she raced across the floor, she could hear the key turning in the lock. She shook the handle and kicked the door. She'd been so close to freedom.

Abigail ran her fingers through her hair and tried to calm herself with a deep breath, but she was unable to fight off the reality that she was completely and utterly defeated—and trapped.

Jesse stared at the camera. No way was he going to confess to something he hadn't done, and no way was he going to let anything happen to Abigail. He suspected that once he confessed, both he and Abigail would be killed, anyway.

Frisk leaned over the camera and clicked on a button. He straightened his back and pointed. "You can sit on that chair right over there."

The sheer arrogance of the man infuriated Jesse.

Frisk's hand fluttered over his gun. The message of the gesture was clear—Jesse had better do what he was told.

Jesse sat down. Agent Frisk stalked over to him. He

pulled a knife from his pocket and cut Jesse free. "We don't want it to look like you were under duress." Frisk pulled his gun and pointed it at Jesse. "That doesn't mean you can try anything."

Jesse massaged his wrists where his hands had been bound. A plan began to come together in his head. The keys were behind him by the monitor. He could get to them before Frisk did, but he probably couldn't get out of the room before Frisk shot him. He threw up his hands and shook his head. "I guess you win."

The ploy was designed to make Frisk let down his guard a little. If he thought Jesse was still fighting, he'd remain vigilant. Shoulders slumped, Jesse moved as though he was going to sit in the chair. Then he turned suddenly and dived toward Frisk. Jesse barreled into him, knocking him to the ground, and got on top of him. Jesse reached for Frisk's gun.

Frisk landed a blow across Jesse's jaw that made his teeth hurt and his eyes water. If Frisk pulled his gun, he'd have the upper hand. Still stunned from the hit he'd taken, Jesse lifted his arm to strike Frisk's head.

Frisk managed to angle away before Jesse's fist made contact with Frisk's head. Again Jesse reached for the gun. His fingers wrapped around the barrel. He pulled it out of Frisk's pocket. Frisk lunged for Jesse, grabbing the hand that held the gun.

As the two men struggled for possession of the gun, it went off. The bullet hit the ceiling, causing dust to rain on them.

The two men wrestled, falling to the floor and rolling around. Jesse's back rammed against the legs of the counters. He rolled to one side just as Agent Frisk came at him. Frisk had dropped the gun somewhere.

Jesse's eyes scanned the floor as a surge of adrenaline renewed his strength. He jumped to his feet and went after Frisk, landing a blow to his face and then his stomach. He kicked the backs of Frisk's knees, which caused him to tumble to the dusty floor. Jesse hit Frisk on the back of the head, knowing that would knock him out. Frisk collapsed to the floor on his stomach.

Jesse's heart pounded against his rib cage as he whirled around and grabbed the ring of keys Frisk had set on the counter. Once again, he searched for the gun but didn't see it. Frisk's phone was in the pocket that faced the floor. He couldn't waste any more time. Frisk would regain consciousness in a few minutes.

The door was unlocked. He stepped outside into the evening light.

He scanned the area around him that consisted of one functioning drilling rig and several inert ones, along with some metal buildings and trailers. He turned back to face the door and stared at the ring of five keys. The second one he tried fitted the lock. Frisk had a phone on him and could call for help, but they'd have to break him out unless someone else had a key. Jesse reasoned that it would buy him a few valuable minutes.

Now to find Abigail.

He hurried along the outside of the corrugated metal building that contained the monitoring equipment.

He ran toward the next building. A man with a gun walked by, headed toward the parking lot. Jesse hurried around the side of the building to keep from being spotted. A large shed blocked his view of much of the facilities. The room where Abigail was being kept had no windows.

He sprinted to the other side of the shed. The buildings that he could see were all trailers with windows. As he ran, he had a view of the parking lot. There were three cars and a truck parked there. One man was still perched on the hood of a car, holding a gun.

He darted around the trailers, crouching and pressing close to the siding in case there were men inside who could spot him and sound the alert. Once he was around the trailers, he saw a large rectangular building. Part of it had windows, and he could see the remnants of a cafeteria inside. But the far end of the building was windowless. He ran toward the cafeteria.

When he looked over his shoulder, he saw at least four men running toward where Frisk was trapped. So the alarm had been raised. That meant he had only a few minutes before they came looking for him.

He hurried into the cafeteria, past the dusty tables and serving areas. He ran through what must have been an industrial kitchen at one time, though it looked like all the appliances had been salvaged or stolen. He homed in on a door at the far side of the kitchen.

He pounded the door with his fist. "Abigail, are you in there?"

Seconds ticked by. No answer. His heart sank.

Then he heard a faint voice. "I'm here, Jesse."

He let out a breath as his spirit soared. She was okay. "I'm going to get you out." He stared down at the keys, eliminating the one that had locked Frisk in the control room. The first one he tried didn't budge the lock. "Hang in there."

"What else can I do?"

He appreciated her wry sense of humor in the face of such danger. The second key he shoved into the hole didn't budge, either. His heart raced. The men were probably already searching the property, headed in this direction. He pushed the third key in the hole and it turned. He swung the door open.

Abigail fell into his arms. He felt a sense of relief as joy surged through him. He kissed her hair and her forehead. "You have no idea how glad I am to see you."

She tilted her head. She gazed at him as though looking right through him to some deeper place. "I think I do, 'cause I feel it, too."

Her eyes were wide and welcoming, her lips slightly parted. For a moment, time stood still. He pressed his lips on hers.

He kissed her as a sense of melting and being on fire at the same time washed over him. He deepened the kiss, holding her close. He pulled back, still reeling from the power of the kiss. "You have no idea how much I want more of that. But they're coming for us."

She reached up and rested her hand on his cheek. "I understand. Let's get out of here."

He took her hand and led her into the cafeteria. Through the windows, he saw two men headed in their direction.

"There's a side door over there," she said.

They hurried outside. The door slammed behind them just as a gunshot sliced through the wood of the door. They raced toward a defunct oil rig, slipping behind it for cover.

Jesse stared out at the vast flat landscape with rolling hills in the distance. If they ran that way, they would probably be caught. "We need to get to that parking lot and grab one of those cars." Jesse took in a breath as his heart raged.

Abigail nodded. "You know the lay of the land. Lead the way."

A gunshot pinged off the metal of the rig. Without a word, both of them hit the ground and crawled toward the next thing that would provide cover—a dry drainage ditch.

The dimming light of evening provided them with a degree of cover as they inched their way along. Still, the two men had seen them in the cafeteria and behind the drilling rig. It would be just a matter of time before they searched the drainage ditch.

Up ahead, Jesse could make out a twisted pile of metal that created a sort of overhang they could hide under if they both curled into a tight ball. The men who were searching for them had not had time to grab flashlights, though they might have phones that had one. So far, they hadn't used it.

Abigail rolled into the tight space first, and then he slipped in beside her. In order to fit, they both had to lie on their sides. Jesse squeezed in close to Abigail, facing her. Their noses were nearly touching. He scooted his legs in so they wouldn't be visible.

Above them he could hear the men shouting at each other, their voices growing louder and then fading. When the voices sounded like the men were quite far away, Abigail reached up and rested her palm on Jesse's cheek. The silent show of affection and support warmed him all the way to the marrow of his bones.

The voices grew louder. He was so close to Abigail he could feel her body tense with fear.

The men were directly above them.

"They must have run off," said one of them.

"Out toward that field, do you think?"

The first man took a moment to answer. "They're just going to run into a big pile of nothing and a bunch of coyotes if they go out that way."

The second man laughed. "Yeah, but they don't know that."

"Better get back to the boss man and figure out how we'll mount up a search."

Jesse listened to the sound of the retreating footsteps. The night fell silent.

Abigail lifted her head, indicating she thought they should move.

Jesse shook his head. Best to wait and listen.

She leaned close so she could whisper in his ear, "My legs are cramping."

His hand rested on her shoulder. Being this close to her reminded him of the power of the kiss they'd shared. The intensity of the moment still had him reeling. Yet the kiss had been impulsive, at a moment of intense danger. Had he kissed her because he loved her, or was it driven by fear because he thought he might lose her?

Even though they remained physically close in the tight quarters, he could feel himself retreating emotionally. He knew from experience that loving someone came at a high cost and an extreme risk of pain. Was he ready for that?

He rolled away from her. "I think the coast is clear." Jesse crawled out from beneath the tight space and got to his feet.

Abigail stood up beside him.

A light flashed suddenly in his eyes. "Fooled you," said the voice of the thug holding a gun on them.

SEVENTEEN

Abigail's heart revved into overdrive as she shielded her eyes from the intense light.

She could only discern the man's silhouette, but it was clear that he had a gun aimed at her.

Each word the man uttered seemed to be dripping with violence. "I knew it was just a matter of time before you got uncomfortable down there. I wasn't about to go crawling around in that mess. Guy could get all cut up from the metal that's been tossed in there," he said. "Now, both of you put your arms in the air and crawl out of that ditch." The man aimed his flashlight, indicating the path they were supposed to take.

Now she saw all the metal and debris that had been dumped in the dry riverbed that they could have been cut on. Abigail stepped in front of Jesse.

The man with the gun backed up as they got closer to him. He stumbled on something and flailed his arms to keep from falling. The gun flew off in the darkness somewhere. Jesse, who wasn't even to the bank of the riverbed, lunged toward the man. The two of them got into a fistfight.

Jesse could handle himself.

She searched for the gun. It was hard to see anything in the dark. She dropped to the ground and felt around with her hands in the area where she thought the gun had landed. Nothing.

When she looked over at the two men, Jesse was on top of the other man, punching him.

In the little bit of moonlight, she saw something shiny in the grass and crawled toward it. It was the thug's phone. It must have flown out of his hand when Jesse tackled him. He'd been using the flashlight on it.

The two men continued to wrestle. The thug crawled on top of Jesse, hitting him in the face and chest. Abigail switched on the flashlight on the phone and directed it into the thug's eyes. He drew a protective hand up to his face, which allowed Jesse to punch him in the stomach. The man drew his knees up to his chest. Jesse got out from under him and hit the thug several more times.

The other man grew still. Jesse leaped to his feet. "He'll be out for a little while." He ran toward her. "Come on, we don't have much time."

"Are we going back to get one of the cars?"

"They must have sent other guys in other directions looking for us. There can't be that many men still around." He grabbed her hand and they ran.

His touch brought the memory of the kiss they had just shared like a flood washing over her. They were two people from two very different worlds. Probably nothing could come of it. The lights of the barracks came into view. There was no time to think about what the kiss meant.

They ran past the nonfunctioning drilling rig and the cafeteria, not seeing anyone. Jesse slowed down and took cover behind the first structure they encountered, a cargo container that was probably used for storage. Both of them angled around the side of it to have a view of the rest of the camp. From where they were, she could not see the parking lot.

One man holding a rifle stalked through the barracks. They both pressed against the cold metal of the container as the man marched past them, preoccupied with speaking into his phone.

They hurried toward the next building, a storage shed. She followed Jesse around to the side of the building. Both of them crouched low. Only two cars remained in the parking lot. That meant the others were out looking for them.

Heart racing, Abigail glanced around. So far, they'd only seen one armed man. The thug who had ambushed them at the drainage ditch would be waking up within minutes and running back here to sound the alarm. She was glad she'd taken the thug's phone. It bought them some time. There was no way to calculate how many men were still here, but at least they weren't dealing with an army.

Jesse pressed his back against the building. "You have that guy's phone."

"Yes." She held it up.

"See if Frisk's name is on there," Jesse said.

She looked down and scrolled through the list. "It isn't here. They all have code names." She remembered seeing the names on Larry's phone when he'd kidnapped her down the road from Dale's cabin. "I think Frisk's code name is Ernie and that's how he's listed. Frisk is the one behind all of this, right? Are you thinking taking him into custody might help clear your name?"

"If we get out of here, he'll be out of the country by

the time I can get the DEA to listen to me," Jesse said. "This might be my only chance. You could get to one of those cars and get out of here safely. I'll take care of this."

"We're in this together, Jesse. I'm not going to leave you." Abigail reached over and squeezed his hand.

Both she and Dale had seen the contents of the hard drive. That might help his case, too. If Dale was alive.

He leaned close to her. "I know there are a lot of maybes to this plan."

She stared out at the parking lot. She noticed a man standing in shadows at the edge of the lot. It was probably his job to watch the parking lot. Even just getting away in one of those cars held huge risk. Staying together was their best chance for escape.

She took in a deep breath. "I say we try to lure Frisk out."

Jesse's heart swelled with affection. "You have no idea what this means to me." He held out his hand. "Give me the phone. I think I can imitate the voice of that guy who jumped us back at the drainage ditch."

She placed the phone in his hand. "How exactly are we going to get the jump on Frisk?"

"I'll get him to give up his location by saying I have target two—that's you—in custody."

She nodded. "Okay."

"Hopefully he'll tell us his location. I'll bring you to him. You stand in front of me so his view of you is blocked. When I touch your back, get out of the way and I'll jump him."

"Got it," she said.

Her courage amazed him. "I'm so going to take

you out for a nice meal when this is all over with," Jesse said.

"That would be great, Jesse. Just to do something ordinary."

He thought he detected a hint of sadness in her voice. Maybe she was wondering if the kiss was a mistake, just like he had. If they weren't working to stay alive, was there even enough of a bond to keep them together?

Jesse clicked on Ernie's number.

"Tell me you have good news." The voice on the other end of the line was Agent Frisk.

Jesse cleared his throat. "We have target two." The important thing was that his voice not sound like his own and that he keep his words to a minimum to avoid suspicion.

"And target one?" Frisk's voice was filled with accusation.

"He's still at large."

"Bring her here. I'm in the control room. Maybe we can use her to lure him out. I don't think he'll leave without her. He's in love with her."

Frisk's last words echoed in his brain. When Jesse had seen Abigail on that camera, Frisk must have picked up on Jesse's feelings even before he had. He was a trained agent. It was his job to be able to read people. Yet he was unsure of his own heart.

"Craig, are you still there?" Frisk sounded impatient.

Jesse glanced over at Abigail. "Yes, I'll bring her in." Still in a state of shock, he clicked off the phone, then reached for her as fear washed over him. "I don't know what I was thinking. You don't have to do this."

"Let's end this once and for all." She stood to her feet. "I'm choosing to do this, Jesse."

There was no arguing with her.

They hurried through the barracks, darting from building to building, aware that if they were spotted someone might sound the alarm to Frisk.

They moved toward the door on the square metal building where Frisk was.

Abigail slipped in front of Jesse, and he stood directly behind her. She opened the door so Frisk would see her.

Jesse could not see him, could only hear his raspy voice. "Well, look at you."

Abigail must have managed to play the part of the frightened captive.

"You won't trick Jesse into coming for me. He's long gone. The authorities will be here any minute," she said.

Jesse stared at Abigail's long blond braid. *Way to go, Abigail.* He had to hand it to her. She played the part well. Her comment not only fed Frisk's fear, but would also continue the ruse that Jesse was not standing right behind her.

"Good work, Craig," said Frisk. "I'll take it from here."

Abigail dived to the floor. Jesse lunged toward Frisk, whose eyes had gone round with surprise. He reached for his gun. Jesse distracted him with a left hook to the jaw that seemed to stun him into momentary paralysis. Frisk's hand hovered over his gun but he didn't grasp it.

Abigail crawled across the floor, grabbed a piece of metal and hit the backs of Frisk's knees with it. He collapsed to the ground. He dived toward Abigail, wrapping one arm around her neck and then pulling his gun, pointing it at her head.

"She'll die if that's what you want," said Agent Frisk.

All the air left Jesse's lungs as he struggled to get

a deep breath. His gaze rested on Abigail, who panted for air, but her eyes were not filled with fear. He saw resolve there as she nodded. Somehow, they would find a way to get the upper hand.

Jesse put his hands in the air. "Okay, just back off of her."

Frisk shoved the gun toward Abigail. "Drop that piece of metal."

Abigail let her weapon fall to the floor.

Still on his knees, Frisk waved his gun. "Both of you, go over there and sit down."

Jesse moved toward the corner on the opposite side of where the door was. Abigail crawled in that direction, as well.

Even though he had the gun, Frisk was in a defensive position. Once he stood up, he would be harder to overpower.

Frisk winced as he struggled to get to his feet. Abigail must have hurt him when she hit him. In the seconds Frisk tried to stand, he and Abigail lunged toward him together as if on cue. Abigail picked up the piece of metal again.

Jesse reached toward Frisk's hand that held the gun. They struggled. Abigail landed another shot to Frisk's legs. The man collapsed to his knees. Jesse yanked the gun away from him.

He pointed the gun at Agent Frisk. "On your feet, hands in the air."

Abigail searched the control room, recovering a piece of wire. "Hands in front so I can tie them up."

Frisk complied with a sneer on his face. "My men will come for you. You'll never get out of here."

Jesse searched Frisk's pockets, finding a ring that

contained car keys. "Come on, we don't have much time."

With Frisk in tow, they hurried out to the parking lot.

Abigail helped Frisk into the back seat and then slipped into the front passenger seat. Jesse gave her the gun to hold on Frisk while he rifled through the keys until he found the one that fitted.

"See, I told you they'd come for me." Frisk tilted his head toward the barracks, where two shadowy figures made their way toward the parking lot.

Heart racing, Jesse shifted into Reverse. Another man ran toward them from the edge of the parking lot. He must have been patrolling the area. The thug raised a pistol and took aim.

Frisk laughed. "I told you so."

Jesse pressed the gas and cranked the steering wheel. The other two men had reached the edge of the lot and were running toward the other car.

In his rearview mirror, Jesse saw the thug who had been patrolling the lot raise his gun. "Get down."

The back windshield shattered.

Jesse sped toward the edge of the parking lot. "You all right?"

Abigail's voice remained steadfast. "Yes, we're both good."

As he pulled out onto a dirt road, the other car was right on their tail. He had no idea where they were going or how far it was to civilization.

He pressed the gas, going as fast as he dared on the dirt road. They were still a long way from safety.

EIGHTEEN

Abigail kept the gun pointed at Frisk. His eyes became narrow slits as he stared straight ahead, his jaw set tight.

A breeze floated in from where the back window had been broken.

The other car was so close its headlights made her shield her eyes.

Jesse kept his focus on the road while he spoke. "Abigail, you still have that phone."

"Yes." She pulled it out of her pocket.

"Try calling Dale." Jesse recited the number to her.

She clicked in the numbers as Jesse spoke them. The phone rang once. Twice.

"No one is going to help you," said Agent Frisk.

"You be quiet."

The phone rang a third time. Then she heard a voice, faint and warbled. "Dale, is that you?"

She heard her name but not much else. It had to be Dale. He was alive.

A reply came. She could only decipher a few words. But it was clearly Dale's voice. It sounded like he was standing inside a fan.

She heard only one phrase clearly. "Stay on the line."

"Okay, I'll keep talking."

"He must be working with someone who can figure out where we are by bouncing the signal off the cell phone towers," said Jesse.

Abigail continued to talk about all that had happened to them, though she could not discern much of what Dale said in response.

Jesse came to a crossroads, taking a sharp left turn. When she glanced out the windshield, she saw lights in the distance. Maybe it was a small town.

The other car stuck to their bumper. Another shot was fired. It pinged off the outside of their car.

Abigail's heart raced. A little shaken, she kept talking into the phone but kept the gun pointed at Frisk.

Just as Jesse turned onto a paved road, the other car came up beside them.

One of the men had crawled into the back seat of the other car. He rolled down the window and pointed a pistol at them. Abigail slipped down in the seat. Jesse swerved. Their car rolled out onto the grass beside the road, bumping along.

Once he was back on pavement, Jesse did a sharp turn, headed in the other direction. Up ahead, Abigail saw no lights, just a vast, dark emptiness.

A voice came to her across the phone, clearer than before. "Abigail, are you still there?"

"Yes, Dale, I'm still here, but I have no idea where we are."

The reply was garbled and then the line went dead.

Abigail glanced out the broken back window. Changing direction had put some distance between them and the other car, but it looked like they were going back to the middle of nowhere.

The other car had gotten turned around and was headed toward them, traveling at a high speed.

She didn't need to tell Jesse the pursuers were gaining on them. She saw his nervous glance in the rearview mirror.

Her heartbeat drummed in her ears as her whole body tensed.

Jesse pulled onto a shoulder on the road and turned around again so they would be going toward the light of civilization. The other car swerved into their lane, headed straight toward them in a deadly game of chicken. The other car drew even closer, still not getting into the other lane.

"Are they crazy?" she said as her throat went tight with terror. A head-on crash would not serve anyone.

Abigail held her breath.

The other car sped toward them.

Jesse cranked the wheel to avoid a crash, bumping along the rough terrain that surrounded the road. The other car rolled off the road and came to a stop.

Jesse slammed on the gas.

Agent Frisk glanced behind him as the thug's car grew farther away. He hit the bottom of her hand so the gun flew out of her grasp. She glanced at the gun, which had landed in the front seat. He wrapped his bound hands around Abigail's neck and pressed his arms against her throat. "Let me out or she dies."

Abigail fought to break free, clawing at Frisk's hands as she gasped for air. Black spots filled her vision.

"Let her go." Jesse reached over, pounding and scratching at Frisk's arms.

The car swerved and fishtailed. Jesse slowed in an effort to regain control of the car. The grip around her neck loosened just as the car flipped. She had the sensation of being airborne before sliding along on hard ground. The car came to a standstill.

She fumbled around for the seat belt latch but couldn't find it. She was upside down and trapped in the car. She felt light-headed, dizzy. Jesse said something to her. She responded automatically, though she hadn't totally comprehended his words.

She heard doors creaking open. Men shouting. A strange whirring sound she could not identify filled the air. When she looked over to the driver's seat, Jesse was gone.

Jesse crawled out of the car. Frisk was trying to make a run for it. He wouldn't be able to run very fast with his hands bound in front of him. He'd told Abigail where he was going, but had she been coherent enough to comprehend?

Down the road, the thugs' car got closer. Jesse watched as Frisk made his way toward the road and the ride that would allow him to escape justice.

Overhead in the distance, Jesse saw the flashing lights and whirring blades of a helicopter. Had one of Frisk's cohorts been able to bring in more manpower just like they had done on the mountain?

Jesse darted toward Frisk as he drew closer to the thugs' car. Jesse's legs pumped hard. He closed the distance between him and the other agent. He leaped through the air, bringing Frisk to the ground.

The thugs' car slowed as it approached. Gunshots filled the air around Jesse.

"You will not live to see another day," Frisk said

through gritted teeth as he was lying on his stomach with Jesse on top of him.

Gunshots directed at the car came from the helicopter, which hovered just above the ground.

Jesse pressed his hand on Agent Frisk's neck to keep him from getting away.

A hand cupped his shoulder. "I got this." Jesse was overjoyed to hear Dale's voice. "Go take care of Abigail."

Jesse ran back toward the overturned car. He hurried around to the passenger side, yanked open the door and reached inside. He unclicked Abigail from her seat belt and dragged her out.

He held her in his arms, touching her face and her hair. "Abigail?" He drew her limp body close to his chest.

"I'm okay." Though her voice was weak, the sound of it made joy wash through him.

She gripped his collar and gazed up at him.

Beautiful, brave Abigail. He touched her face. "We made it. Everything is going to be okay."

He hoped he was right about that, that his name would be cleared and he could go back to doing what he loved. What would happen between him and Abigail, however, was still uncertain.

NINETEEN

Abigail's stomach tensed as she surveyed the tables in the restaurant. It had been almost a week since she'd returned to Fort Madison after giving her testimony about what she had seen Frisk say and do, and what she'd seen on the destroyed hard drive.

She'd made the decision to move back to Idaho. There was nothing left for her here in Fort Madison.

Jesse stood up and waved at her from a corner booth.

His text to her had been quick and to the point. I'm back in Fort Madison and would like to take you out to dinner as a thank-you for all you did for me.

Seeing him made her heart leap.

She'd thought that once they were no longer together, once they didn't have to depend on each other to stay alive, the intense feelings she had for him would subside. But time and distance had done nothing to erase her affection for him.

He stood up and pointed at the other side of the booth for her to sit.

She sat down. He smiled at her.

"Are you back to being an agent?"

"It looks that way. Frisk didn't confess. But some

of his cohorts rolled on him. The testimonies you and Dale gave helped a lot. They're working on searching the plane for evidence. That's why I'm back here."

So he hadn't just come back to Fort Madison to take her out to dinner. She struggled to hide her disappointment. Maybe she had been entertaining fantasies that he didn't share.

"Good, so your life is back to what it used to be. And the aloe vera plant. How is he doing?"

Jesse laughed. She liked the little crinkles around his eyes when he smiled. "George was glad to see me, as always."

Abigail laced her fingers together and rested her hands on the table. Sharing small talk with Jesse made her aware of the chasm inside her. "Thank you for keeping your promise and taking me out to dinner." She wanted there to be more between them than small talk. She looked into his eyes, searching. Did he want that, too?

"It's the least I could do for you, Abigail. Considering all you went through for me," he said.

"It was scary at times. But I kind of like the adventure of it all."

"Seriously, you should think about becoming an agent."

"I never would have thought my life would go in that direction…until I met you." The longing she felt was like a wave crashing over her. Being with him now made her realize that she loved him. She wanted to be with him.

"I'm glad to hear you say that." He reached down on the seat of the booth and placed an odd-looking package on the table. It was a six-inch cube wrapped in a fast-food wrapper and held together with electrician's tape. "It's for you. I had to MacGyver the wrapping together with what I had in my car. I thought you would appreciate that."

She laughed. "Very clever." She reached for the package. When she got the wrapping off, she stared at a box that had at one time been for the bulb in a car headlight. "Okay?"

"Open it." His voice lilted with a note of excitement. "Remember when I met you, my initial impression of you was all wrong because of what Brent had done to you. Just 'cause the wrapping isn't classy doesn't mean what's inside will be trash."

She rested her hand on top of the box. "And my first impression of you was totally off, too. You are an honest man, a good man." She met his gaze. The warmth in his eyes made her heart race.

She opened the box.

Jesse cleared his throat. "I don't know where our lives will end up. I'd love it if you became an agent and we worked together. But I would be completely open to rethinking my life and living somewhere where you could be a guide."

Inside the large box was a smaller box. She pulled it out.

"The only thing that matters to me, Abigail, is that I'm with you."

She opened the box, which contained an engagement ring.

"Oh, Jesse." Joy flooded every cell of her body. "Yes, I will."

"You didn't let me ask the question." He reached over and covered her hand with his.

"The answer is still yes."

He laughed and leaned across the table, gesturing for her to come closer. She leaned in. He touched his hand to her cheek and pressed his lips on hers, sending a charge of electricity through her.

When she'd walked into the restaurant, her world had seemed upside down and empty. Now, with Jesse, it was right side up and full of possibility. She looked forward to a lifetime with the man she loved.

* * * * *

If you enjoyed this story, look for these other books by Sharon Dunn:

Hidden Away
In Too Deep

Dear Reader,

I hope you enjoyed the exciting and sometimes harrowing adventure that Jesse and Abigail experienced as they sought to clear Jesse's name. Both Jesse and Abigail were on an emotional adventure, as well. They both had thought their lives were going in a particular direction and both suffered losses that derailed them. For Abigail, it was Brent's betrayal. And for Jesse, it was the loss of his wife after only a short marriage. Like most people, they made plans that involved college, career and marriage. Nobody factors in loss that is bound to happen sooner or later.

When my husband died, I was forty-nine years old. I had been married since I was twenty-two. My world turned upside down. Before he got sick, Michael and I had begun to talk about the travel we would do together once the kids were grown. We were making plans to grow old together. Like Abigail and Jesse, I assumed life would move in a certain direction. Loss and the derailment it causes is not easy. I am just so grateful that I have a God who is my refuge and is faithful despite life's suffering and losses.

Sincerely,

Sharon

COMING NEXT MONTH FROM
Love Inspired® Suspense

Available February 5, 2019

AMISH SAFE HOUSE
Amish Witness Protection • by Debby Giusti
After her son witnesses a gang shooting, single mom Julia Bradford and her children are sent to witness protection in Amish country. But can former cop turned Amish farmer Abraham King keep them safe?

PROTECTING HIS SECRET SON
Callahan Confidential • by Laura Scott
When his ex-girlfriend, Shayla O'Hare, returns to town with a little boy in tow and a target on her back, private investigator Mike Callahan vows to protect them. And discovering the child is *his* son makes him even more determined to stop the assailants.

FATAL THREAT
Emergency Responders • by Valerie Hansen
Back home after a mission trip, nurse and EMT Sara Southerland learns that her cousin's death might not have been an accident—and now someone wants *her* dead. Her old friend—and crush—fire captain Adam Kane is the only one who can help her survive.

TAKEN IN TEXAS
McKade Law • by Susan Sleeman
Called to the scene of a deadly crime, Deputy Kendall McKade must track a kidnapper, and the culprit is determined to silence her. With help from Detective Cord Goodwin—her former boyfriend—can she stay alive long enough to solve this case?

JUSTICE AT MORGAN MESA
by Jenna Night
Someone will do anything to keep Vanessa Ford from uncovering the truth about her father's murder—but she refuses to stop searching. Police lieutenant Levi Hawk volunteers to work with her on the investigation...and keep the killer from making her his next victim.

ROCKY MOUNTAIN SHOWDOWN
by Victoria Austin
In her remote mountain cabin, Laura Donovan and her daughter are trapped between a forest fire and a killer. Park ranger Seth Callahan comes to their rescue, but can he get them off the mountain safe and sound?

Get 4 FREE REWARDS!

We'll send you 2 FREE Books plus 2 FREE Mystery Gifts.

Love Inspired® Suspense books feature Christian characters facing challenges to their faith... and lives.

FREE
Value Over
$20

SPECIAL EXCERPT FROM

Love Inspired

SUSPENSE

*When her son witnesses a murder, Julia Bradford and
her children must go into witness protection with the
Amish. Can former police officer Abraham King keep
them safe at his Amish farm?*

*Read on for a sneak preview of
Amish Safe House by Debby Giusti,
the exciting continuation of the
Amish Witness Protection miniseries,
available February 2019 from Love Inspired Suspense!*

"I have your new identities." US marshal Jonathan Mast
sat across the table from Julia in the hotel where she and
her children had been holed up for the last five days.

The Luchadors wanted to kill William so he wouldn't
testify against their leader. As much as Julia didn't trust
law enforcement, she had to rely on the US Marshals and
their witness protection program to keep her family safe.
No wonder her nerves were stretched thin.

"We're ready to transport you and the children,"
Jonathan Mast continued. "We'll fly into Kansas City
tonight, then drive to Topeka and north to Yoder."

"What's in Kansas?"

Jonathan pulled out his phone and accessed a
photograph. He handed the cell to Julia. "Abraham King
will watch over you in Kansas."

Julia studied the picture. The man looked to be in his midthirties with a square face and deep-set eyes beneath dark brows. His nose appeared a bit off center, as if it had been broken. Lips pulled tight and no hint of a smile on his angular face.

"Mr. King doesn't look happy."

Jonathan shrugged. "Law enforcement photos are never flattering."

Her stomach tightened. "He's a cop?"

"Past tense. He left the force three years ago."

Once a cop, always a cop. Her ex had been a police officer. He'd protected others but failed to show that same sense of concern when it came to his own family. The marshal seemed oblivious to her unease.

"Abe is an old friend," Jonathan continued. "A widower from my police-force days who owns a farm and has a spare house on his property. He lives in a rural Amish community."

"Amish?"

"That's right."

"Bonnets and buggies?" she asked.

He smiled weakly. "You'll be off the grid, Mrs. Bradford. No one will look for you there."

Don't miss
Amish Safe House *by Debby Giusti,*
available February 2019 wherever
Love Inspired® Suspense books and ebooks are sold.

www.LoveInspired.com

Looking for inspiration in tales
of hope, faith and heartfelt romance?

Check out **Love Inspired**® and
Love Inspired® **Suspense** books!

New books available every month!

CONNECT WITH US AT:

Facebook.com/groups/HarlequinConnection

Facebook.com/HarlequinBooks

Twitter.com/HarlequinBooks

Instagram.com/HarlequinBooks

Pinterest.com/HarlequinBooks

ReaderService.com

Love Inspired®

Inspirational Romance to Warm Your Heart and Soul

Join our social communities to connect with other readers who share your love!

Sign up for the Love Inspired newsletter at **www.LoveInspired.com** to be the first to find out about upcoming titles, special promotions and exclusive content.

CONNECT WITH US AT:

Facebook.com/groups/HarlequinConnection

 Facebook.com/LoveInspiredBooks

 Twitter.com/LoveInspiredBks

LISOCIAL2018